Reconciling the Consequences

Ravager Knights MC Book 2

M.E. Thornwood

Midnight Dreaming Publishing

Midnight Dreaming Publishing P.O. Box 312 Elburn, IL 60119

Interior design by Atticus

Book Cover by Covers by Jules

Edited by Maine Woods Editing

ISBN 978-1-962688-03-1

ISBN 978-1-962688-02-4 (ebook)

CONTENTS

Content Warning   V

Dedication   VII

1. Chapter One   1

2. Chapter Two   5

3. Chapter Three   11

4. Chapter Four   17

5. Chapter Five   26

6. Chapter Six   43

7. Chapter Seven   54

8. Chapter Eight   64

9. Chapter Nine   68

10. Chapter Ten   75

11. Chapter Eleven   94

12. Chapter Twelve   102

13. Chapter Thirteen   117

14. Chapter Fourteen   121

15. Chapter Fifteen   141

16. Chapter Sixteen   150

17. Chapter Seventeen   164

18. Chapter Eighteen   180

19. Chapter Nineteen   186

20. Chapter Twenty   191

21. Chapter Twenty-One   216

22. Chapter Twenty-Two   232

23. Chapter Twenty-Three   240

24. Chapter Twenty-Four   254

25. Chapter Twenty-Five   261

26. Chapter Twenty-Six   274

Coming Soon   279

Also By   281

Acknowledgements   283

About the Author   285

Reconciling the Consequences is book two of the Ravager Knights MC series. This is the second book in a series and book one must be read before this one.

It will end in a cliff hanger with the HEA at the end of book 3. This is a Why Choose novel, meaning the main character will not choose between her love interests. This novel has BDSM themes and on page negotiations.

If rough sex, praise and degradation, and angry alpha males that fly off the handle is not your cup of tea, please don't read. This is a work of fiction intended for an 18+ audience.

To the Booktok Girlies,

Sometimes you just need a Harley man to throw you around a bit.

Chapter One

PAIN. THAT WAS ALL Johnathan "Mayhem" Taylor knew. Fists pummeled his torso unchecked. He brought his arms up to block his head but left his torso exposed.

He deserved every punch. Every kick. Every damn hit that pummeled him. He deserved it all.

"Come on, asshole." Derrick "Devil" Halson growled. "Fight back you pussy."

Johnny swung out blindly with a gloved fist. It connected with a thud, and a slight hiss emanated from Kevin "Rockstar" Adams, his best friend and brother in the MC.

Another punch caught Johnny in the ribs. "That all you got?" Kevin goaded. "Where'd the big man go? The one who called our girl a whore?" He spat through clenched teeth.

Johnny opened his eyes, a growl ripping from his chest. He jabbed with his right fist, knocking Kevin across the jaw. Johnny blocked with his left arm as Derrick aimed another punch to his rib cage.

"There we go." Derrick nodded, clapping his fists together.

The crowd surrounding the regulation MMA octagon was massive and cheered loudly from the stepped concrete platforms around the room that gave everyone a great view of the ring. The Pit—the building that housed the ring they were currently fighting in—was the holy grail of the Ravager Knights compound and hosted MMA fights twice a year.

Today was not about that, though. Today was about a wrong that needed to be righted. A respect paid to his best friends, his brothers.

He had screwed up *again*. He had wronged them and their woman.

Now she was lying in the hospital fighting for her life while they had no way of knowing if she was even alive. Someone had tried to kill her. Someone had tried to kill their woman in her own home.

It was unacceptable. They had left her unprotected.

They had put her in danger by keeping her in the dark. They had left her defenseless while issuing a club-wide lockdown. They had called in clubs from almost every state because their club was under attack. The Pit was full of out-of-town brothers from charters across the country. San Jose, Oakland, Las Vegs, Salt Lake City, Cheyenne, Boulder, Omaha, Cedar Rapids, Texarkana, Shreveport.

Johnny had put her in danger. He was acting president of the Ravager Knights Mourningside charter while his father, Mac "King" Taylor, sat in county jail accused of crimes he did not commit: racketeering, embezzlement, money laundering, and fraud.

Someone had framed him using a company that he had registered forty years ago.

Life was in shambles around Johnny, but it had been his responsibility to protect his club, his brothers, his woman.

He had failed.

A sucker punch landed across his right eye, and his head spun from the impact.

This was their way, though. He would let his brothers publicly beat his ass to take a piece of that disrespect back.

He had told them both what happened to her as soon as he'd returned from her house, after he had pulled her out of the burning building and left her on the front lawn. He'd also informed them of the body he had found with multiple bullet wounds at the bottom of her basement stairs.

Derrick had decked him right away, but Kevin had held Derrick back from delivering the ass-kicking that Johnny deserved. For the second time in the last two months, Kevin had told Johnny, "I'll see you in the ring."

Here they were a full twenty-four hours later, on display for all their brethren, to right a wrong. Johnny honestly didn't know if it would even be enough; his grievance had been too steep.

Another punch landed across his jaw; his bottom lip caught between his teeth and split open, blood flying. He groaned and finally snapped out of his pity party. "Fucking finally." Kevin snapped after Johnny got a punch in.

Things moved quickly after that. Johnny and Kevin had both trained in mixed martial arts as children. Their fathers had both been in the club and the Marines together; they saw the added benefit of starting their boys young.

Kicks and jabs, combo after combo, dodges and hits, the three of them continued until the sweat was pouring down and they were barely able to stand.

Johnny would not be the one to end this fight—it would be up to Kevin and Derrick. They had called the fight, they were the ones slighted. *Two of the three I wronged, anyway.*

He would have to grovel for the rest of his life, and even then, he didn't think that would be enough for what Kara deserved.

Chapter Two

Marcos Candela lounged in an uncomfortable hospital chair at Mourningside General Hospital in central Mourningside, Illinois. His knee bounced anxiously as he scrolled through his phone.

As next of kin, he had received the phone call from a nurse when his sister, Kara Carmichael, had been brought in three days before with multiple injuries.

Marcos was still wrapping his mind around the fact that his baby sister had been attacked in her home. She had somehow fought off her attacker and killed him—a man that was easily twice her size.

Kara had paid the price, though. Her face was a swollen mass of bruises and horrendous coloring, she had a broken wrist and a long cut on her arm that had needed stitches. She also had broken three ribs and punctured a lung. A drain tube had been inserted in her chest to reinflate her lung and decompress the chest cavity. She had needed surgery to repair the torn ACL in her left knee. She'd even managed to break two fingers on her right hand, most likely from a punch that landed the wrong way on her attacker, if Marcos had to guess.

Marcos could barely look at his baby sister in the hospital bed. Along with the chest drain, she had IV for fluids and antibiotics and a catheter. At one point there had also been a blood bag to replace all she'd lost.

According to the doctors, she had gotten extremely lucky. Nothing in her face had been broken despite the gruesome bruising. She did have a minor concussion, but considering everything else, it was almost inconsequential.

The police had been by to speak to him and check on her. Marcos had advised them that they could speak to his sister when she was well and truly healed. Or not, if he had his way, since most of the cops in this town were crooked as hell. The two officers had taken one look at his leather cut and puffed out their chests with a macho bravado that grated on Marcos's nerves.

Marcos was restless—he hated the not knowing. Why the fuck had someone tried to kill his sister? He'd questioned the police, but all they had said was that she had been attacked in the house and managed to fight back and shoot the guy with his own gun.

It had only led to more questions from both him and the cops. Was she working on a case that would have someone looking to hurt her? Was she dating anyone that was violent? Who was the man in her house? The neighbors had reported that someone had carried her out, but no one had gotten any distinguishing features other than that he was probably male.

Marcos had nothing to give the police either. He and his sister weren't close, though they kept in touch. He didn't know the first thing about her work, and he purposely kept a lot of his life away from her.

She didn't even know he was in the Devil's Psychos Motorcycle Club.

There was so much they both hid from each other, and he couldn't blame her. She called to open up to him about dating not one but *three* men at once—together—and he had lost his shit and basically called her a whore.

That had been the last time they spoke.

She had been attacked three days later.

Here he was three days after her attack, still waiting for her to wake up.

Marcos's list of regrets was a mile wide when it came to his sister, and it started on the day she'd been born. He'd been ten years old, and his single mother had worked hard to support them. Back then she was still turning tricks, still looking for a husband, and most of the time Marcos was left alone with a new baby.

His mother hadn't been mother of the year by any means, but she had tried. She had kept a roof over their heads, put food on their table and clothes on their backs. She might have been a little desperate for love and always looking for a Romeo to sweep her away from a life of poverty, but she'd worked her ass off, both figuratively and physically, to the very end.

As Marcos got older, Kara was his sidekick most evenings. At five years old she was smart as a whip and would call him out for cussing too much. He often dragged her around the Creekton Villages—the large low-income apartment complex on the south side of Creekton—where they lived, exposing her to people and situations she had been far too young to handle.

At five years old she'd watched a neighbor overdose and die in front of her. After that Marcos had vowed to get her out of that life. At fifteen he dropped out of school and started working full time. He convinced their mother that Kara needed to go to a private school instead of the local public school in the ghetto of Creekton.

It had been the best decision he had ever made despite the fact that it had led him to a life of crime. Kara had thrived in the private school in Mourningside and had gone off to college. When her father had magically appeared her junior year and handed her Harvard and the means to pay for it, Marcos couldn't begrudge her for wanting to go or for wanting a relationship with her father.

The fight Marcos had with her over it was just another entry in the long list of regrets when it came to Kara. It had changed everything between them. Kara went from telling him everything to only sharing big events, usually after the fact.

There was a knock at the door, pulling Marcos out of his musings. Marcos looked up to find his best friend and brother Jason "Stone" Langford standing in the doorway. He had on a pair of dark wash blue jeans and a red button-down shirt that was left open over a black T-shirt. A throwback to the '90s, if ever there was one, he even had a silver chain around his neck.

His dirty blond hair was styled in a messy bedhead look, and his steely gray eyes pierced right through you. He had a barbell through his left eyebrow, and that was just the start of his piercings.

"Hey," Marcos muttered, nodding his head. "What's up?"

"How is she doing?" Stone's voice was deep. He wasn't one for talking. He could say a lot with just a look.

Marcos turned to his sister and found no change. He sighed and shook his head. "The same."

Jason's stoic expression didn't change. Marcos braced himself for whatever his best friend was about to say. "Pres called a meeting. Heat's picking up between us and the Ravager Knights. The Knights have emissaries from almost every charter in the country in town. They're flooding the streets and blocking our trade routes."

Marcos growled and stood up. "All because of that push into Buffalo Creek?"

Jason gave a curt nod.

Marcos shook his head and ran a tattooed hand over his buzzed black hair. "Alright." He nodded and headed toward the door.

Stone paused. "She gonna be OK on her own?"

"She's been on her own all her life."

Chapter Three

*I*T HURTS. *EVERYTHING HURTS. Make it stop.*

Pain radiated across her body. It was the first thing Kara Carmichael knew as she struggled to consciousness. Her body felt heavy, her head cloudy.

There was an incessant beeping that felt like it was driving a spike through her head.

She struggled to open her eyes, her lids heavy.

The beeping increased.

She groaned and her heart raced as she began to panic. Why couldn't she open her eyes? Everything hurt.

The noise was driving her crazy. She wanted to throw something at whatever was making it.

She snapped her eyes open and took a deep breath. She looked around: white room, lots of monitors. Hospital.

The door to her right opened, and she turned her gaze that way. "Afternoon Miss Kara," an older black woman greeted with a smile. "Great to see you awake. How we doing today?"

Kara took a deep breath and tried to calm her racing heart. "Hurts," she answered with a heavy rasp. "Water."

"I imagine it would, dear," the woman continued. "My name is Momma. I'll be taking care of you. Why don't we get you sitting up and we can call the doctor. We can see about getting you some ice chips until then."

She bustled about, tending to machines and wires. Once Kara was sitting, Momma took her blood pressure. "That handsome young man just left. He's been here the last three days, not leaving you for anything."

Kara's eyebrows furrowed.

"Buzzed black hair, full goatee, soulful chocolate eyes, muscles and tattoos for days," Momma drawled, a smirk on her face.

Kara cracked a smile. "My brother."

"That's what he said." She grinned. "Like I said, he just left a bit ago, but that man has been by your side the last three days straight."

Kara frowned, thinking about everything that happened. Her eyelids felt heavy again and instead of fighting it, she went with it.

The next day, Kara sighed after the doctor left. Her prognosis was good, all things considered. The drainage tube in her chest could be removed—she'd passed his coughing test for her lungs. The bandage on her chest had been replaced with a clean one, as had the one on her left knee—it was currently elevated with pillows and a large immobilizing brace.

Her right wrist was in a cast as well as her thumb, pinky, and ring fingers. She had landed a punch wrong on Randall Diggins's face when he had attacked her, breaking her last two fingers. The fall down the basement stairs broke her wrist and several ribs—one punctured her lung. And judging by the jagged cut she'd received on her left forearm, she might have snagged a nail on the stairs during her fall. The nasty looking wound had required twenty stitches to close.

She hadn't looked at her face yet, but it hurt. She vaguely remembered a knee to the nose. Her concussion had been mild she was told, and her nose hadn't been broken, so she'd take that as a win.

She had been unconscious in the hospital for three days. Today was the fourth day of her stay, and the doctor said he wanted to keep her for observation for another two or three days.

Kara had agreed. She had no idea the state of home—she vaguely remembered the smoke and fire. She wondered if she even had a home to go back to. Even then, it wasn't safe. Randall Diggins might be dead—she hoped he was dead—but it didn't change the fact that her father had hired his goon to kill her.

After he had warned her off poking further into Case Holdings and the Granger case, and called her a whore, he had *still* hired someone to kill her. Whatever she was going to find digging into Mac Taylor and Case Holdings, her father *did not* want her to uncover.

It only made her want to dig deeper. Now that she didn't have to worry about going against her father—since he'd made it clear that his loyalties lay only with himself—she was free to continue to dig.

And dig she would.

As soon as she got out of the hospital.

She sighed and racked her brain, trying to think of everything she remembered from that night. She needed a pen and paper. She hit the call button for the nurse. "Yes dear?" Momma's smooth voice came through the intercom.

"Momma, can you bring me a pen and paper please?"

"Of course, dear."

Kara stared down at the notepad in front of her. On one page she wrote out her multiple injuries. She even had Momma take pictures and email them to Kara's private email. She didn't have her phone any longer, but she could check her email when she got her things back.

She listed out the surgeries she had needed and the recovery time she was looking at, the physical therapy she would be starting once she hit the fourteen-day post-surgery mark for her knee. Then she started listing the things she remembered about the fight. She recalled thinking her Chinese food was being delivered only for the front door to open before she could reach it.

The fight had happened so quickly. Diggins had had her on the ground and stunned immediately. She had managed to get away and grab a knife from the block in the kitchen. She sliced him once before she had been overpowered.

They had scuffled again, and when she went down that time, her foot had been caught between his, and she heard the pop in her knee—her ACL snapping. Diggins had kneed her in the face right after that, most likely giving her the concussion.

She had been dazed and in pain, so the details were fuzzy. She had backed away from him, trying to find a way out, when she bumped up against the basement door. She had struggled to her feet and managed to open the door only for Diggins to attack again. They had scuffled at the top of the stairs, and she'd landed a couple of well-placed elbows to his gut and face, and down he went.

Her downfall was not moving fast enough to avoid his leg striking out and sending her sprawling down the stairs.

She was missing memories, though; something more had happened in the basement. When had she gotten the cut on her arm? How had her house caught fire? She kept thinking she saw Johnny there. Had Johnny been there? Did he carry her out? Why?

After she'd gone by the clubhouse to break up with Johnny, Derrick, and Kevin and let them know her father would be taking over the Granger Ltd. case against Mac, Johnny had been the most vocal. He'd been livid. He had called her a whore and played into every single self-conscious thought she'd had while dating the three of them.

Her heart hurt, thinking of them. She wanted to call them. She wanted one of them to hold her, to hear Derrick's goofy chuckle when he laughed at his own jokes, see Kevin's bright smile when he saw her walking toward him at the office, or even hear Johnny's sarcastic Princess nickname when he thought she was being a little too spoiled.

She missed her guys and vowed she would see them again.

Chapter Four

JOHNNY WAS WORKING ON his F-250 in the garage at the Ravager Knights' compound. The large lot had multiple buildings. It housed their clubhouse, a sprawling three-story building with multiple dorm-like bedrooms upstairs and a full bar and restaurant downstairs. They served the public, but you had to be a friend of the club to continue to come back. Also in the compound were the garage where they ran their legit auto repair shop, a long and sprawling storage shed, half of which they rented out to tenants, and, at the back of the lot was the Pit.

Kevin was giving Johnny a hand, change the oil in the open bay of the garage. Derrick sat off to the side of the garage messing with the radio.

It was Friday morning, and most of the clubhouse was quiet still. Most of their out-of-town guests didn't get up until noon. Johnny was grateful. He needed some time with just his two best friends and brothers. It was long overdue.

"We need to figure out this shit with the Devil's Psychos, man." Kevin groaned. "This lockdown shit is getting old."

"Agreed." Derrick called from across the garage.

Johnny shot him a look but nodded at Kevin. "I know, man."

"And Kara." Kevin added.

Johnny shook his head. They had already had their time in the ring over this. What more was there to talk about? It was dead in the water anyway. She broke up with the three of them. "I don't see how there's anything to talk about. She ended things, remember?"

"That wasn't Kara." Kevin shook his head vehemently. "I *know her*," he stressed. "Something happened to spook her. Someone said something, got to her."

"Yeah, man." Johnny snapped, turning his back to the open bay door. "Someone got to her! They attacked her! They tried to fucking kill her!" His voice rose with each sentence. "That's exactly what we were trying to avoid by putting fucking distance between us and her last week! The trade routes are already under attack from the Psychos. We already lost a brother, and then our fucking girl was attacked in her home!" Johnny panted as he continued his tirade. "No. There's nothing else to discuss about Kara. She's better off without us."

Johnny stared at Kevin, but Kevin and Derrick were looking past him with disbelieving expressions on their faces.

"Doesn't she get a say in that?" a female voice asked behind him.

Johnny froze, his shoulders tensing. Her voice was raspy and low, but he'd recognize her sweet voice anywhere. Kara was behind him. He whirled around, his heart clenching in his chest as the air whooshed from his lungs like he'd been sucker punched in the gut.

She looked rough. Her blond hair was a mess, her blue eyes no longer sparkled, as deep bruising surrounded them. She also had a split lip, but that was inconsequential compared to the black and blue bruising covering her face.

Her right arm was in a cast from just below the elbow down to her hand. It included her thumb, ring, and pinky fingers. It was also bright-ass pink. There was a bandage over her left forearm, covering a good portion of it from elbow to wrist. She leaned heavily on the side of a car; her left knee and most of the leg were in an immobilizing brace.

She stood before them in socks and hospital scrubs, looking like she'd walked through hell...and survived.

"Kara." Johnny breathed, unable to move.

She assessed him, as he had her. He knew he looked rough; he hadn't slept much in the last week since she had been attacked. Knowing she was in the hospital fighting for her life and being unable to go to her had killed him. Then there were the bruises on his face and his own black eye from the fight with Kevin and Derrick.

"Holy shit," Kevin muttered from behind Johnny.

"Baby girl, fuck." Derrick groaned and went to her.

Kevin and Derrick pushed past Johnny, and he let them. He stepped aside so his brothers could go to their girl. They moved slowly, as if they were afraid they would startle her. "Can I?" Kevin asked softly.

She nodded as tears lined her eyes. She rested her forehead against Kevin's chest while Derrick circled behind her and wrapped his arms around her waist. His mouth immediately found the sensitive spot on her neck, and she let out a low moan.

Kevin ran his fingers through her messy hair and held her gently. "Kara," he muttered, at a loss for words.

Johnny hated that she was so fucking hurt, hated that his brothers were heartbroken seeing her like this. He hated that his greatest failure in life had been not protecting her. His heart ached. He wanted to go to her, pull her into his arms, and beg for her forgiveness. But he knew she wasn't safe with them.

She needed to be as far away from him and the club as she could get. Only then would she be safe. "You shouldn't be here," Johnny said, his voice low.

"Dude, what the fuck?" Kevin snapped, whirling around. Kara leaned sideways on the car as Kevin faced Johnny, his brown eyes blazing as he glared.

Johnny ignored him and kept his eyes on Kara. Her blue eyes were alight with a fire he hadn't seen the last time she was at the clubhouse—over a week ago, when she ended things. "Oh no,

Johnny? Why's that?" She shot back at him, raising an eyebrow. *She's going to make me say it, isn't she?*

He steeled his spine and his heart for the words that would drive her away. She needed to be safe, and safe meant not being associated with him or his club. "You don't belong here. Never did. Just another—"

"Fuck you," she snapped before he could finish. "You don't think that. Not in the slightest." She shook her head. "You wouldn't have pulled me out of my burning house if that were the case."

"I don't know what you're talking about." He denied it immediately.

"The fuck you don't." She glared. "Why were you there that night? Huh Johnny? And don't feed me some bullshit line either about not being there. I remember you."

Johnny's heart raced and his cock kicked in his jeans. Fuck, he loved it when she got all riled up; it turned him on so fucking quick. She was so fucking beautiful, even now. "I think you hit your head. Maybe you should go back to the hospital or go check into a hotel room." He deflected.

Kara's glare was glacial, her baby-blue eyes ice-cold as she stared at him. "You really are an asshole," she snapped.

"I've been tellin' ya, Princess," he shot back. "You don't want to listen. But in case you haven't noticed," he continued, "we're a little busy around here." He motioned around the compound as a whole. "You don't belong here. So run on back to your *Daddy*," he stressed, "and go back to your ivory tower. Forget you ever slummed it with the likes of us."

She laughed sardonically and shook her head. She stepped away from the car and leaned back against Derrick, letting him take her weight. She was pale and looked like she was growing weaker by the minute. "I would, you see," she rasped, "but I can't. I'm not safe anywhere. That man that broke into my home and attacked me? His name was Randall Diggins. He's been my father's hit man for decades."

"What?" Kevin breathed, shoulders tensing.

Johnny stared at her in disbelief.

Derrick tightened his hold on her hips.

"Yeah." Kara nodded. "My father tried to kill me because he didn't want me digging into the case anymore. Even after he threatened that he would have the three of you thrown in jail for bullshit cases, *even after he called me a whore* for sleeping with the three of you and made me break things off, he still sent his guy to kill me." She laughed and shook her head. "All because my father is the one framing Mac. Mac and Vince started Case Holdings together forty years ago, but my father is the only one who used it. He's been embezzling money from his own firm and clients for decades."

Johnny's mouth dropped open. He was utterly speechless.

"What the actual fuck?" Kevin voiced what Johnny was thinking.

"So you don't want to break up?" Derrick questioned.

She shook her head slowly, looking between Johnny and Kevin, before she looked back over her shoulder at Derrick. "No, I never wanted to break up. He threatened to put you guys in jail if I didn—"

Derrick cut her off midsentence with a kiss. He kept it gentle by the looks of it, but Kara still groaned and eased back. "Sorry," he muttered.

"Don't be," she mumbled. "Everything hurts." She closed her eyes and rested her head back on Derrick's chest.

"Kara." Johnny breathed, taking a tentative step toward her.

He wasn't the only one. "Kara!" Kevin shouted at the same time Derrick cursed and caught her as she passed out.

Derrick gingerly scooped her up bridal style. "Well, now what?" He looked at Johnny.

Johnny rubbed a hand over his buzzed blond hair. "Lay her in the back seat of the truck. We'll take her home." He sighed.

"Seriously?" Kevin asked, shooting him a look.

"The clubhouse is full. You want her bunking with one of them? No, we'll take her home with us. She'll be safer with us anyway," Johnny said.

Derrick didn't need to be told twice. Johnny opened the back door for him, and he climbed inside with Kara cradled in his arms.

Once he had her situated on the back seat, he snaked the middle seat belt around her waist before he climbed out and closed the door.

"Um, excuse me." A male voice called out from the open bay door.

Johnny whirled to see a gangly looking man with shaggy hair and glasses standing in front of the F-250. The guy was holding several plastic bags marked with Mourningside General's logo. "What do you want?" Johnny grunted.

"This is all her stuff from the hospital." The man held up the bags.

"Who the hell are you?" Johnny stalked toward the guy.

"I'm just an Uber driver." The guy squeaked, raising his hands in surrender.

"Jesus." Kevin hissed and headed toward the guy. He pushed Johnny aside and grabbed the bags from the kid. "Thank you."

"Yeah, no problem." The kid squeaked again before he ran for his little Nissan Altima.

Johnny sighed and cleaned up his mess. Thankfully they had finished with the oil change already.

Johnny didn't glance back at Kara until he was driving down the road with Devil and Rockstar riding in formation behind him, but then he wished he hadn't—her skin was ashen and she looked dead.

He kept his eyes on the road and focused on moving forward. It was all they could do now.

K ARA WOKE UP IN complete and utter agony. She groaned and whimpered; her ribs and knee were on fire. They throbbed to the beat of her heart and only picked up tempo the more distressed she became. "Easy, baby." Kevin's deep rumble came from her right.

She popped her eyes open to find she was in an unfamiliar bedroom. The room had gray walls with white trim and a large picture window half covered by navy-blue curtains. The king-size bed she was lying on was soft beneath her. She'd been tucked tight beneath the sheets and blankets and propped up against a mountain of pillows, her left knee elevated under another stack.

She turned to find Kevin lying next to her on the bed, his head propped on his hand as he faced her. "Hurts." She whimpered.

"I've got your meds right here." He nodded and held out a handful of pills.

The sight of the three horse pills in his hands was a welcome relief. He handed them to her and then held up an insulated stainless steel cup, her cup—the one with the straw that she carried everywhere. She took a sip of the ice-cold water and groaned. It tasted divine.

She took another sip and tossed back her pills, grateful to be propped up on the mountain of pillows. She breathed through the pain and hoped the pills would kick in fast. "Where are we?" she asked, closing her eyes.

"Our house," Kevin answered. "We took you home with us."

Kara didn't know what to think of that, then decided she wasn't going to think about what it might mean. Those were problems for another day. She hummed in response.

"I read through your discharge papers," Kevin continued, his voice thick. "We'll keep up with your meds so you don't feel the pain like this again."

"Please." She whimpered, a tear slipping down her cheek.

"Fuck, baby." Kevin groaned. "I'm so sorry. I should have been there. You shouldn't have been alone."

Kara snapped her eyes open and looked at Kevin, taking in his disheveled appearance. His black hair was past due for a trim; the usual well-kept locks were in complete disarray. He had dark circles under his eyes, as if he hadn't been sleeping, and his right eye had the yellow bruising of a healing black eye.

"Why didn't you call me?" she asked, thinking back to the week before her attack. The three of them had practically ghosted her after their weekend sexathon at her house.

Kevin reached out and grazed his fingers gently over the skin of her face. "I wanted to. I wanted to every single day."

"But you didn't." She snapped.

"You're right, and you have every right to be pissed about that." He agreed, nodding.

Kara rolled her eyes and turned her head away. She hated when men did the whole, "your feelings are valid" thing. No fucking shit, bro. She knew she had a right to be pissed off; the placating just pissed her off more. "Leave me alone," she said. She didn't have the energy to deal with whatever bullshit explanation he was going to come up with.

"I'm sorry, Kara. If you would just let me explain," he started again.

"No, Kevin." She snapped, opening her eyes. "I expected better from you. Me and you, we started this thing together, just the two of us. I thought I meant more to you."

Kevin sat up carefully so as not to jostle the bed. "I know. I fucked up. I should have called you and told you what was going on. With the shit going on with the club, we didn't want you to get involved. We thought it would be better, *safer for you*, if we kept you out of it."

Kara glared at him. "You can keep me out of the club shit by *calling me*. You can TELL ME you have club shit going on that you can't talk about. I'm not a fucking idiot, you know. I know the three of you do shady shit."

Kevin only nodded.

She shook her head in disbelief. "I don't feel good, Kevin." She sighed, resigned. "I just want to sleep."

"Alright." He solemnly agreed.

She closed her eyes and gritted her teeth as he slowly got off the bed. When the door closed behind him she let out a shuddering breath and let the tears fall. She had to breathe through her pain, had to focus on not sobbing. Her ribs screamed in agony with every breath she took.

She focused on her breathing, used the tool kit her therapist had given her to combat her panic attacks. She breathed in for four counts and held it for seven counts, then slowly released it for eight counts.

She continued her breathing until she felt calm and her eyes grew heavy. She dozed off, feeling drained and emotional.

~*~

Kara was pulled from her sleep sometime in the middle of the night. It was dark in the bedroom. "Kara." Derrick's soft voice was to her right.

She turned her head to find him sitting on the bed next to her.

"You need to take your pills," he explained and held out his palm with three of her pain meds.

She nodded and took the three pills with her left hand. He held the straw to her lips, and she took a sip of water before she tossed back the pills and swallowed. She felt better this time than she did the last time she woke up.

"Sleep, baby girl," Derrick murmured and kissed her forehead.

She didn't need to be told twice and quickly drifted back to sleep.

Her stomach hurt the next time she woke up. She realized she had been taking pills on an empty stomach and groaned. Thankfully she wasn't in too much pain. She also really needed to pee and realized she couldn't remember the last time she had used the bathroom.

She looked to her right and saw Kevin there again.

He was lying down, facing her but still sleeping. He startled awake when she shifted. "You OK?" he asked immediately. "What do you need?"

She'd smile at his attentiveness, if she weren't so annoyed with him. "I need to pee." She sighed, realizing she would need help hobbling to the bathroom at least. "And maybe food?" she added, giving him a bone.

"We can do that. Let's get you up." He rolled off the right side of the bed and circled around to her side.

She kicked the blanket off of her with her right leg and then looked around and tried to figure out how to do this.

"Alright, let's take it slow," Kevin said. "I'll move the pillows here," he put his hand on the stack under her left knee, "and you can slowly swing your legs off the bed. Use your good arm to roll into a sitting position at the same time."

"I don't have a good arm," she muttered, but she followed his directions and rolled onto her left elbow. The stitches in her forearm didn't pull too badly, and she found that it was relatively easy to sit up—mostly pain free. She wasn't jostled at least, and nothing felt too excruciatingly painful. She had a feeling all of that would change once she was standing.

"Your discharge papers had tips for maneuvering," he said as he came to her left side. "Why don't you hold on to my arm here," he looped her stitched arm through his so she'd hold his elbow like he was escorting her down a red carpet. "I'll help you a little, but you'll do most of the moving yourself."

She nodded, understanding what he was getting at. She put more pressure on her good leg and, using her stitched arm, leaned forward and slowly stood up. "Well shit." She breathed once she was standing. She was technically able to put her full weight on the injured leg twenty-four hours after surgery, but her doctor had recommended only doing so for short periods of time to help prevent swelling and possibly reinjuring herself.

She held Kevin's elbow and hobbled slowly toward the en-suite. The large bathroom was fully remodeled and modern, decorated beautifully with a freestanding vanity and white granite countertop. The room was done in a wash of grays and white that matched the bedroom.

Once Kara was confident that she could use the countertop to hobble over to the toilet, she turned to Kevin. "I've got this," she said softly.

He nodded almost reluctantly, his hand rubbing the back of his neck. "Alright. I'll get you some food. Any requests?"

"Toast with jelly, if you've got it? Maybe some sausage or bacon?"

"I can do that," he agreed. "Yell if you need anything."

Kara took her time relieving herself and getting cleaned up. When she stood at the sink washing her hands, she noticed her travel toiletry bag. Inside was all her stuff. That's when she paid attention to her surroundings: her hairbrush was on the counter along with her toothbrush and her makeup bag. She looked through the glass of the shower and saw her full-size shampoo, conditioner, and bodywash with loofa. Someone had raided her house for her things.

She wondered what that meant for the state of her house. How much damage had the fire caused?

Kara brushed her teeth and ran her hairbrush though her messy blond hair the best she could with three broken ribs. There was no way she'd be able to put it in a ponytail, not with her hand and wrist in a cast and the other arm covered in stitches. She would need help for that.

She was dying for a shower.

She would have to settle for food, though.

She opened the bathroom door just as Kevin walked back into the bedroom carrying a plate of food and a glass of milk. She smiled at his thoughtfulness. She waited while he set everything down on the nightstand, then came back around to help her hobble over to her bed.

"Whose bedroom is this?" she asked, realizing the smell of sandalwood was faint.

"Johnny's," Kevin replied as he helped her lower back down on the bed.

She narrowed her eyes at him. "And whose idea was that?" she snapped.

"His." Kevin shrugged.

She didn't even know why she was surprised. Johnny was a controlling asshole on a good day; why would she expect anything different from him? "Of course it was," she retorted.

A smile tugged at the corners of Kevin's lips, but she ignored it. Once she was situated back in bed and her leg was propped up again, he handed her the plate of food. Her stomach growled as she took in the two pieces of wheat toast buttered and slathered in strawberry jam. There were two pieces of bacon and two sausage links as well.

"Thank you." She sighed softly, accepting the plate.

"No problem, babe." He pressed a kiss to the top of her head.

"I'm still upset with you," she added.

"I know."

"OK."

After Kara ate breakfast and took more pills, Kevin handed her the remote to the big-screen TV that was mounted on the wall across from the king-size bed. It was one of those fancy ones that looked like it was a picture frame, not a TV.

Kara had her choice of streaming services to browse through and settled on a random Avengers movie. She knew she would probably doze off, as the meds made her drowsy. She would hate them if she weren't in so much pain without them.

The next time Kara woke up, Derrick was lounging in the bed next to her. He was playing a game on his phone, and a different

Marvel movie played on the TV. "I'm mad at you," she informed him by way of greeting.

A deep laugh rumbled out of his chest. "I'd expect nothing else, baby girl," he replied with a nod, unaffected.

She rolled her eyes. "I'm hungry," she informed him.

He smirked. "You're cute when you're crabby."

She glared at him, but it was more in annoyance than anything with heat. "Why did you ghost me last week?" she asked instead.

She watched his face fall as his playful smile dropped. "Kara." He sighed, finally looking up from his phone and turning to her.

She stared at him, taking in his shoulder-length brown hair and his thick, bushy beard. His bright green eyes were guarded. She noticed the dark circles under his eyes. Like Johnny and Kevin, he sported a black eye, though his and Kevin's were nowhere near as bad as Johnny's had been.

He at least looked like he'd been put through the wringer. "I'm sorry," he started, and she waited. "I'm sorry that we didn't reach out. That I didn't reach out. We could have texted more and called at least once or twice. There was no reason for us to completely *ghost* you even though we had shit going on. In the end, it would have been safer for you to know what was up so you would know to watch out for yourself... When Johnny said he'd pulled you out of the house..." Derrick shook his head. "Honestly babe, we all spent the last week thinking that one of our enemies tried to kill you because of the shit we have going on right now."

Kara stared at him confused. "The club shit?" she asked.

He nodded. "I know you don't want to know a lot, but we're beefing with another club right now; trade routes have been disrupted. One of our guys, a brother, was killed last week," Derrick explained.

Kara's heart stopped in her chest. The pain in his green eyes was deep; it cut her to the core. "Derrick," she murmured and ran her hand through his shaggy beard. "I'm sorry you lost a brother."

He nodded solemnly. "Thank you, but I'm not telling you to excuse our actions, but because of that, we should have kept in touch, at least let you know what to look out for. Shit, not left you alone *period*."

"I've been on my own most of my life." She shrugged. "I'm used to it."

Derrick shook his head; his green eyes were sad. "You shouldn't have to be, baby girl."

She shrugged and turned away from him. She focused on the TV and let the conversation go.

He turned to the nightstand, grabbed a tray he had sitting there, and handed her a plate with a sandwich, chips, and her pills in a little cup.

They were going to kill her with kindness, trying to make shit up to her. And she was going to let them.

Kara woke slowly when she awoke next. She took notice of the changes in the room first. The TV was off, the overhead fan was on, the curtains had been closed tightly—though she could still see light peeking through the slight gap and around the top edge. The room had been plunged into cool darkness.

It felt amazing.

She turned to see who was in bed with her and froze when her eyes landed on Johnny. His eyes were closed as he lay on his back. His chest was bare, and he had crawled under the covers but kept his distance in the king-size bed.

It was too dark in the bedroom to make out the bruising on his face, but she had seen it—he had two black eyes and a busted lip. His face had been almost as black and blue as hers, though his was healing faster. He was already on the yellowing stages, while she was just starting to turn from black to blue. She had some green tinged areas at the edges, but she still had several weeks of recovery ahead of her.

Kara sighed when her bladder made itself known as the reason she'd been woken. She tossed the sheet and blankets off and swung her legs around; the stack of pillows that were used to elevate her knee had been kicked away in her sleep.

She was able to bend her knee slightly without pain, and from reading her discharge papers, she really should be trying to use it more regularly at this point and only elevating and icing it to alleviate swelling.

She sat up slowly and only gasped slightly from the tinge of pain that emanated from her ribs.

"Need help?" Johnny's thick voice startled her.

She jumped and hissed, grabbing her ribs to stem off the pain. "No," she grumbled.

"Suit yourself." He grunted, his breathing already evening out again.

She rolled her eyes and stood up. She took her time, using the wall to hobble toward the bathroom. All the while, Johnny slumbered peacefully in bed.

She closed the door softly behind her, though she felt like slamming it loudly to wake him up. She wasn't that petty, though, even if he got under her skin constantly. *He had to have chosen to put me in his bedroom for some reason, right?* She knew the guys lived together. Derrick or Kevin could have easily had her bunk with them.

Kara did her business in the bathroom and eyed the shower wistfully. There was a built-in bench on the back wall and a detachable showerhead. Her stomach grumbled for dinner, but a shower sounded wonderful. It had been a full week since her attack and the surgery to repair her knee.

She felt gross, and the urge to shower overwhelmed her. She was still in the hospital scrubs she was sent home in, as her clothes had been destroyed at the hospital. The smart thing would be to wait for Kevin or Derrick to be around and have them help her. Her cast made it difficult to do much of anything, while her left arm was covered in twenty stitches, and she had a couple in her side from the chest drain as well.

It was unavoidable: she would need help.

She sighed and finished using the bathroom. She would have to speak to Johnny and find out if Kevin or Derrick was home. She opened the bathroom door and noticed the clock on the night-stand next to Johnny read 8:05 p.m. That would explain why there was still light coming from behind the curtains.

"Johnny?" she asked softly. He must be tired if he was in bed at eight on a Saturday night.

"Yep," he replied without opening his eyes.

"Is Kevin or Derrick home?" she asked, tentatively.

"Nope."

She frowned and glanced back at the shower longingly.

"What do you need?" he asked.

She shut the bathroom light off and sighed in disappointment. He was still being a dick, and she really didn't want to ask him for help. She limped around the bed and headed back to her side.

"Kara." Johnny groaned and sat up slowly. "What did you need?"

"Nothing," she said.

Out of the corner of her eye she saw him run his hand over his messy blond hair. "Look," he started, "this isn't going to work if you can't tell me what you need."

"I don't *need* anything," she snapped at him. "I just wanted a shower." She shook her head. "I can wait till tomorrow for Kevin or Derrick to get back."

"They won't be back tomorrow or Monday. You're stuck with me," Johnny admitted.

She opened her mouth to reply but was at a loss for words. *Why they said anything to me? They left me here with him?* It was bad enough that she had trust issues with them, now she *really* was going to have trust issues.

Was communication really *that fucking hard* for these guys?

She felt tears welling in her eyes and tried to blink them back, but they fell before she could stop them. She leaned her shoulder against the wall at the foot of the bed as she tried to stifle a sob.

"Fuck," he muttered.

She jumped slightly when his hand landed on her shoulder. She hadn't heard him move, but there he was, with her at the end of the bed, pulling her into his arms.

She let him. Despite everything he said that night at the clubhouse, she still loved him. Despite his grumpy attitude, he still cared about her. He still cared enough to pull her out of a burning building and give up his bedroom, or at least share it. Whatever it was that he was doing.

He guided her a few feet over to the foot of the bed. He took a seat and pulled her onto his lap. She was perched on one of his legs while hers dangled between his spread thighs. It was moments like these when their size difference usually turned her on. She loved how much bigger he was compared to her.

All of her guys were bigger than her, but he was the biggest, and he usually made her feel safe. She perched awkwardly on his thigh, unable to really relax against him. She no longer trusted him, and it broke her heart.

She ducked her head under his chin; she didn't want to look at him. The room was dark, and his face was hard to read. She didn't want him to see her so weak, so vulnerable.

"I'm sorry," he said, and she froze, her breath caught in her throat. "I'm sorry that I called you a whore. That I was such a fucking asshole that night. I'm sorry that I made you feel that you didn't mean anything to us... to me," he added.

She squeezed her eyes shut. She didn't want to do this with him right now—she wasn't strong enough. A sob tore out of her, and her ribs ached, but she couldn't stop. The sobs racked her body, and her breathing grew ragged.

Johnny held her tight against him and let her get it out. He pressed kisses into her hair and forehead every so often but kept quiet.

She curled up in his lap, bringing both knees over his thighs. He wrapped his arms around her and held on tight. She sobbed against him until she felt herself grow tired. As her tears slowed and dried up, she let herself drift off against him.

Chapter Six

THE FOLLOWING MORNING SHE woke up alone. She tried to feel the sheets and see how long Johnny had been gone, but the cast didn't really allow for much feeling. She groaned.

She was sore; she'd missed her evening pills. Missed dinner too, by the sound of her stomach. She slowly got out of bed and headed for the bathroom. She used the toilet and cleaned up a bit, brushed her teeth and hair. She refused to look at the shower, despairing of ever getting clean.

She smelled food cooking, so she headed for the door. She hadn't left the room since she'd been brought there. She had no idea where the kitchen was, but she intended to find out.

She opened the door and paused. The house was not what she was expecting. It was one of those two-story houses with a vaulted ceiling and open hallway overlooking the massive living area below. The bedrooms were all along the one side of the house.

Johnny had the master suite with the double-door entrance. There were at least five or six doors on the right of the hall as she headed toward the stairs. The hallway went far past the stairs that looked to be in the center of the house. She wasn't feeling very adventurous, though, and headed for the stairs.

She only paused briefly to think about her knee before she made sure she had a good grip on the railing with her left hand and slowly made her way down the stairs. Her stitches pulled slightly, so she had to adjust her grip as she hobbled down the stairs.

The great room she walked into was massive. The vaulted ceiling had stained wooden beams bracing it, a huge wall of windows that looked out to the park-like backyard, and French doors that led out to a huge back patio that surrounded an in-ground pool.

She continued through the living area and took in the plush leather sofas and recliners. The huge TV mounted high above the fireplace was a focal point in the room, which was done in shades of black and brown with forest green accents throughout. It was beautiful and manly but elegant. She instantly fell in love with the house.

She passed the formal dining table with its massive chandelier and headed to the kitchen space. It was at the far end of the great room, and while it was technically still the same room, she could see it also wrapped around the corner. It had two massive kitchen islands and the largest stovetop she'd ever seen. It even had not one but two pot fillers.

It wasn't your typical white modern kitchen. This one was black and white and had copper accents: black lower cabinets, white upper cabinets, a gray and white marbled countertop, and a white subway tile backsplash with black grout.

There was a huge copper farmhouse sink under windows that looked out to the backyard. A copper range hood was over the massive stovetop. Two full-size double ovens were built into the wall. There was even an industrial size fridge.

In the middle of it all, Johnny was cooking at the stove.

He looked up when he noticed her enter the kitchen. He looked tired, as if he hadn't gotten much sleep. His face was still bruised, but his black eyes had faded to a sickly yellow color. "Morning," he greeted, his voice thick from sleep.

"Morning," she replied softly. She didn't know where she stood with him.

He'd apologized for being a dick essentially, but it had felt almost *underwhelming*, like it wasn't enough. She didn't know how to explain it without coming across as a stuck-up bitch, so she let it go for now. She was hungry and sore, she needed to take her pills, and she still desperately wanted a shower.

She couldn't wait for Kevin or Derrick to return. She had a doctor appointment tomorrow, and she would need to clean up before then.

"Eggs?" Johnny asked.

She nodded absently and took a seat at the kitchen island closest to him. "This place is amazing," she complimented.

"Thanks," he said, glancing around as if he'd grown used to the magnificence and forgot to really see it. "It was the first project we did when we got out of the Marines," he admitted.

Kara's mouth dropped open in shock, and she looked around again. She'd had a feeling he had designed this, but knowing was something different. "Is this your dream house?" she asked softly.

Johnny shrugged and turned back to the stove. "I don't know that I'd call it a *dream house*," he muttered. "But it was something we had talked about a lot while we were deployed. My grandma had left the lot to me. The house that was here wasn't anything special, a small three bedroom from the '50s. We tore it down and built this. We wanted the main focus to be on the backyard. There's five acres."

Kara could only nod as she stared in wonder at the beautiful home. She was startled out of her reverie when Johnny set a plate down in front of her. She jumped and looked up at him. He had the faintest hint of a smirk on his lips.

She ignored him and looked down at the pile of food on her plate: home fries, sausage, bacon, two eggs over easy, and two pieces of toast already buttered and topped with strawberry jam. "Oh my God." She groaned. "This looks amazing."

"Eat up," he said as he headed back to the stove. She watched him dish up his own plate before she tucked into her meal.

Johnny's nerves were shot with every damn moan Kara made as she ate her food. He was a glutton for punishment, though. He watched her pouty pink lips wrap around her fork and wished it was his cock.

"Kara." He sighed, setting his fork down.

She looked right at him, dead in the eye, wrapped her lips around her fork sensually and fucking *moaned* so loudly.

All he could do was close his eyes.

Her giggle was light and airy and sent the blood shooting for his cock.

"Please, just eat," he begged.

"I am eating. After this, though, I'll need your help showering, please," she added in a singsong voice.

Johnny could only squeeze his eyes tighter. This torture was the punishment that he earned, and even then he didn't deserve her. She was already too forgiving. He deserved to be yelled at, beaten, and destroyed for what he'd done to her.

After that, she ate her food in relative silence and ignored him until she was done. "Thank you for cooking," she said and got up and headed for the sink.

He just nodded, unable to reply to her. He could barely look at her; every bruise and cut and injury was a reminder that he had failed her. Failed them all.

He didn't comment when she started rinsing the dishes, though he did watch her. She was still dressed in those hospital scrubs she came home in. Her blond hair was matted in spots down her back. She moved slowly as she limped from the sink toward the stove.

"Leave it. I'll help you shower." He sighed, defeated.

She froze, her back to him.

He watched her and waited. Did she really not want his help? A week ago, it would have been no big deal. He would have carried her into the shower and had his way with her. Not now, though. Everything was fucked up, and she didn't trust him.

"That's OK." She shook her head, her back still to him. "I'll wait for Kevin."

Johnny felt his hackles rise in response to her flippant and dismissive attitude. She really didn't want him to help her. He rolled his eyes. "Sure, you could. But since he and Devil are on a run this week and won't be back until late Thursday, you need to shower. You're starting to stink."

She whirled on him. Her blue eyes blazed with ire. "Still smell better than you," she snapped.

He smirked slowly. "Nah, darlin," he drawled. "Right now? You're pretty rank."

"I hate you." She said it so matter-of-factly that Johnny's heart clenched in his chest.

"You can hate me all you want, Princess." He sighed and stood up. "But you still need a shower."

"I can do it myself," she snapped and stalked out of the kitchen.

Johnny let her go. She would realize really quickly that she had no way to cover that cast. He set his own dishes in the sink along with the pan he used to cook everything in, then he reached underneath to the bag of plastic bags they saved from grocery shopping. He grabbed several bags and a roll of duct tape from the junk drawer and headed for the stairs.

He found Kara sitting on the edge of his bed, staring into the bathroom. He frowned when he saw the tears rolling down her cheeks. "Kara," he murmured softly.

She wiped away the tears slowly, not ashamed of them. "I'd rather Kevin or Derrick was here," she muttered, looking away from him.

A dagger right to the heart. He deserved nothing less.

"I don't know why, though. All they do is lie. At least you haven't done that," she continued forlornly.

"You think I didn't lie? That fucking night you walked in and broke shit off? I had to lie through my fucking teeth to get you out of there. You just gave me the ammunition to do it." Johnny shook his head, watching her eyes as she stared blankly at him. He hated this dejected and beaten down Kara.

Where the fuck is her fiery spirit that sends my blood racing as she busts my balls?

She snorted and shook her head.

He gritted his teeth and moved in front of her. "I lied that night. I said I should have given you to my brothers, that—"

"That I 'was just another whore that walked through these halls'?" she questioned, her voice low as she looked up at him, throwing his words back in his face.

Johnny gritted his teeth. "I told you, I lied that night. You have never been just another whore to me."

She stood up abruptly, and he was forced to step back. "Fuck you, Johnny. You are such an asshole. You don't even know how fucking seriously you fucked up."

He narrowed his gaze at her. "I think I have a pretty good idea," he answered.

She snorted and shook her head. "Really? Because you fucking used my insecurities against me. You ASKED me what my limits were. I told you I couldn't handle being called a whore outside the bedroom, *and you fucking went there, Johnathan!*" she shouted. "Not only did you break my confidence, you broke my fucking heart," she continued, her eyes shining with unshed tears. "I'll never be able to trust you again," she breathed out. She pushed past him into the bathroom and slammed the door in his face.

Johnny gave her twenty minutes in the bathroom before he let himself in with the plastic bags, duct tape, her pills, and a bottle of water. She hadn't started the water yet, nor had she locked the door.

Kara was sitting on the toilet with the lid down in nothing but the top of her scrubs, just staring unblinkingly at the shower. Her pants and underwear were strewn across the bathroom floor, leaving her naked from the waist down, and her knee brace was next to her. She didn't say anything as he reached in and turned on the multiple showerheads. When he was sure the temperature was right, he turned back to Kara to see that she was staring at him warily.

He didn't say anything, just handed her the pills and water bottle. She downed them quickly as he grabbed the plastic bags off the counter. She let him wrap them around her pink cast and tape them closed. She was seven days post-op on her knee. The stitches in her arm, chest, and knee would be coming out tomorrow when she saw the doctor, but the bruising and scarring would remain. Thankfully they wouldn't have to worry about covering the stitches with anything; it would be alright for them to get wet.

She stood up slowly, being stubborn and refusing to ask for help. "Come here." Johnny's voice was gruff as he motioned with his hand.

She hobbled toward him.

Rage washed over him as he took in her bruised ribs and chest—the ugly black stitches in her porcelain skin—as he slowly lifted her shirt over her head. A whimper escaped her lips, and he had to grit his teeth so as to not to growl in anger.

"You can leave," she said, her voice a low monotone as she went to move past him.

He shook his head. "Not happening, Princess. I'm afraid you'll slip on the tile. Despite what you think, I do care about you."

Kara slowed to stop next to him and looked up. The pain in her baby-blue eyes was unreal. "Johnny, I never doubted that for a moment. That's why this hurts so much." She sighed. "I *know* you care about me."

He swallowed thickly.

"I'm sorry too," she said softly and ran a hand across his cheek. "I'm sorry I chose to walk away from you that night. I'm sorry that I broke your heart that night, too."

Johnny closed his eyes.

The rawness in her gaze had his chest constricting. He grabbed her hand before she could remove it from his face and kissed her palm. He opened his eyes slowly to watch her. She was looking up at him with a contemplative stare. "Baby, I will regret that night for the rest of my life," he breathed out, his voice rough.

"Me too." Her eyes closed. He leaned down and pressed a soft, tentative kiss to her lips. She allowed it for a moment before she pulled away slightly.

He watched her mask of indifference fall back into place and had to bite back his retort. He hated when she did that, closed herself off. He especially hated when she did it with him.

He let it go, though. He would have to be patient with her. He would need to work to get back into her good graces, because there was one thing he knew for sure: *he was not done with Kara Carmichael.*

He would never be done with Kara Carmichael.

Chapter Seven

KARA CLOSED HER EYES and let the warm water cascade over her. She didn't want to think about the kiss with Johnny. Didn't want to think about any possible future with him. She was still hurt, and they needed time to work shit out.

She also didn't think about the fact that he was naked and standing three feet from her under the other showerhead in the large shower.

He had claimed he didn't want her to slip on the tile. She had to hand it to him: he was a crafty one. The fact that her dominant hand was in a cast and bag and shouldn't get wet didn't help either. Thankfully the cut on her left arm was healed enough that she could get the stitches damp in the shower. It might have been her better arm, but the ribs on her left side were broken, and the skin stitched from the chest drain. It hurt like a bitch to raise her left arm up to try and wash her hair... she wasn't quite as able to clean herself as she had first assumed.

She was trying to ignore Johnny though. The rage that had simmered in Johnny's blue eyes had set her heart racing. She had had to look away from him. She'd walked into the large shower to distract herself. Now, she was almost frightened what she might find if she did meet his gaze.

So, she asked him something she had thought about since the day she'd first met him. "Why do they call you Mayhem?"

She opened her eyes and immediately wished she hadn't. Water sluiced over his rock-hard muscles, and his blue eyes were hooded and dark, sensual as he watched her. His cock stood unabashedly at attention, hard as a rock.

An amused smirk tugged at his lips as he watched her blatant perusal of his body. She didn't care, he had been hers at one point. Was still hers? She didn't care about the specifics; she was more interested in his story.

"Not much of a story." He shrugged, his voice deep. "I used to be a little more into causing as much mayhem as possible everywhere I went."

Kara frowned; she didn't see it. He was usually so in control of himself. Aside from the night he lashed out at her, he typically was pretty calm and collected. For as much shit as he gave her about being in control of her emotions, he usually had a pretty tight lid on things.

She let it go, though. She turned away from him and reached for her bottle of shampoo. As she turned, her foot slipped and she started to fall. "Shit." She shrieked as she started going down.

She never fell. Johnny's arms wrapped around her, pulling her tightly against him. His arms were like vise grips around her waist. Her head rested against his chest. Her heart pounded. She felt like she'd seen her life flash before her eyes.

"You OK?" he grumbled.

She nodded shakily and held onto his arms. "Thank you."

He squeezed her tighter in response. Thankfully he didn't say "I told you so."

She stayed in his arms for a while before he turned her. Now that her breath was evening out, her ribs were screaming in agony. The almost fall must have jostled them.

"Come on," he muttered. "I'll wash your hair."

She closed her eyes and let him. In the end, he washed her hair twice at her instruction before he put conditioner in and let it sit for a while. He moved on to washing her body with her loofa. He was extra gentle around her bruises and stiches but still got in there and got most of the glue off from all the tape she'd been using.

When she had rinsed her hair and body and was finally done, she continued to stand in the warm water. "Come on," he said and shut off the water on his side of the shower. There was enough space between them that when he pulled his towel from the glass door, he could dry off without getting wet again.

Kara sighed and waited until he had a towel around his waist. Then he grabbed another fluffy towel and held it out for her. She shut the water off quickly and wrung the extra water from her hair.

Johnny came up behind her and wrapped her in the warm towel. He enfolded her in his arms and held her tight. She closed her eyes and savored the feeling. He pressed an open-mouthed kiss to her neck, going straight for the sweet spot that all three of them zoned in on.

She did her best to ignore his lingering. She wasn't ready to forgive him yet. "What am I going to wear?" she asked him.

"You can wear one of my shirts and boxers for now. Then we could head over to your place and grab as much as we can," he suggested.

She nodded slowly. "How bad is my house, Johnny?" she asked the question that had been burning through her mind.

"It's not horrible," he responded, meeting her gaze tentatively in the mirror.

She deflated. "But it's bad?" she concluded, reading between the lines.

He nodded sympathetically. "It's not livable. Most of the back half of the house was destroyed, your office, the guest bedrooms, your kitchen. I've had men stationed there, so nothing should be missing beyond what the fire destroyed."

"My bedroom?" she asked, feeling hopeful.

He nodded. "Mostly untouched. The walls are pretty black—the ceiling was on fire in there. Everything was wet at some point or still is from the hoses, but I'm sure a lot of your clothes are still alright."

She sighed and nodded. "Alright, help me do my hair and get dressed, then we'll go."

Kara gasped as Johnny pulled the truck into her driveway. Tears immediately lined her eyes. Her house was destroyed. Johnny had sugarcoated it. Half the house was just *gone*. Her heart broke into a million pieces.

This was the first place that was ever *hers*. Not something she had to share with Marcos or her mother. Not a room in a place she rented with roommates at university.

No. *It was hers and hers alone.*

"Where was most of your personal stuff?" Johnny asked softly.

Kara snapped out of her daze. "I honestly never had a lot. My mother... single mom, you know? We moved around a lot, and things were lost over the years. I have a couple shoeboxes in those under-the-bed plastic totes from over the years. I have a safety deposit box downtown for anything really important. Everything else was on my laptop..." she trailed off, realizing. "Johnny! My laptop! My phone!"

"Easy," he murmured gently. "They're back at the house. Devil and Rockstar already grabbed them on their first pass through this place, along with your bathroom stuff."

Kara felt her heart calm down a bit. She looked up at Johnny, seeing the calmness he emanated. She nodded slowly. "When was that?"

"The morning after the fire. Once the heat from the fire department cooled off, they came through seeing what they could salvage. When they saw your bedroom mostly untouched, they grabbed anything that looked important. I think they grabbed your bathroom shit on a whim, hoping you would come back to them after the hospital."

Kara frowned. "But not you?" she questioned.

Johnny shook his head and looked away. He stared hard out the windshield of the truck. "I never thought you'd be mine again."

Kara didn't say anything after that. She opened the passenger door of the truck as best she could with her left hand and slowly climbed out. She wasn't wearing shoes. She had on a pair of Johnny's boxers and a baggy, gray Taylor Construction T-shirt that would have reached her knees had she not knotted it at her waist.

"Shit, Kara," Johnny said and quickly jumped out of his truck.

He jogged around to her side, but she was already headed toward the house, barefoot. "There's probably broken glass everywhere," he snapped.

"So find me shoes," she snapped back.

In the end, she found that a lot of her work clothes had been destroyed. Her bedroom had been soaked. The ceiling was black, but she could see holes where the fire had eaten through. Dust and dirt, soot and grime covered everything in a filthy layer.

Her walk-in closet was a nightmare, her silk blouses and dresses ruined. She peeked in some of the garment bags hanging in the closet to find that, though things might be wet, they might be salvageable if she could pull them out quickly so they wouldn't mold.

She saved all her jeans and T-shirts from the closet, but most of her work things were ruined. Her precious high heels, her handbags, belts, all of it was ruined. She knew her homeowner's insurance would or should cover a lot of it, but it was still sad.

Johnny brought extra-large, black contractor bags into her bedroom so she could pack her things. Most of the stuff in her dressers was made of cotton or polyester or nylon—things like yoga pants and pajama shirts, her socks, underwear, and bras, sweaters, and hoodies—and was relatively unscathed.

She dumped everything from her dressers into the bags to take back to Johnny's. Johnny loaded his truck for her while she continued. When her dressers were done, she pulled out all the plastic totes from under bed. Everything looked sealed and dry in the multiple totes, so she stacked them for Johnny and moved on.

She had Johnny grab the totes from the top shelves of her walk-in closet, and then she was done. Anything worth saving fit into the back of an eight-foot truck bed.

"This too." She sighed and patted the heavy cedar chest at the foot of her bed that she was sitting on.

"Seriously?" Johnny groaned.

She just nodded and panted. Her ribs ached; her knee was on fire. She had clearly overdone it, but she had needed to do all of this sooner rather than later.

"Yo, prospect!" Johnny yelled over his shoulder.

Kara jumped when she saw a young kid come running down what was left of her hallway. He was all gangly arms and legs, baggy blue jeans, and white T-shirt. He had a black leather cut with the Ravagers Knight patch on the front.

She bet if he turned around she would see the menacing skeleton in armor holding a scythe. The prospect vest would have the top rocker missing, and the bottom rocker would say *prospect*.

"What's up, boss?" the kid asked, looking very *green*; he couldn't have been older than eighteen or nineteen.

"Let's pick this up." Johnny motioned to the large chest she was sitting on.

Kara sighed and got back up to make room for Johnny and the kid. She stepped out of the way and glanced at the back of the kid's cut. The large dead knight on his back matched the one on Johnny's cut, the cut that no Ravager Knight left home without.

The only time Kara saw Johnny, Derrick, or Kevin without their cuts was on Carmichael and Associates property or inside their home. She assumed they didn't wear it to other jobs either, but she didn't really know.

Her eyes traced over Johnny's back as he and the kid lifted her grandmother's cedar chest and walked it out of what was left of Kara's house.

More than half her house had been destroyed in the fire. The half with the three bedrooms and her kitchen was gone. Her master bedroom and bathroom had been on the opposite side of the house, with the living room between them.

The front door was still standing, as was her front coat closet. She was able to salvage some shoes and coats from there, especially her winter gear. Mourningside, Illinois, was roughly two hours southwest of Chicago, and they felt the same winters.

She had slipped on her running shoes when she walked in the house to make Johnny shut up, but now she was grateful. Her knee was on fire, and the added support from the shoe was nice.

She hobbled toward the front door just as it swung open.

"You OK?" Johnny asked, looking her over.

She shook her head. There was no point hiding it; she wasn't OK.

She wouldn't be OK until they caught her father and locked him away.

Chapter Eight

MARCOS LOOKED AROUND THE Devil's Psychos clubhouse. Once a motel in its prime, it hadn't been kept up over the years and had slowly grown dilapidated. The old restaurant of the motel had been turned into a bar for mostly club members. They did get some hangers-on but not many.

The Devil's Psychos were a rough sort of breed, and they came from rougher neighborhoods than most. Down the Evermore River from Mourningside was the prison city of Creekton, Illinois. Creekton not only housed Mourningside County Correctional but also Creekton State Prison, a maximum security prison for only hardened criminals.

People that lived in Creekton either worked for Mourningside Correctional or Creekton State or they knew someone that did. Kids grew up faster with parents who were overworked and saw too much on the inside.

Marcos had grown up right here in Creekton. His mother had stripped at The Midnight Raven for decades, but even that gentleman's club hadn't made it in the cesspool of a city. Not after the Riverboat Casino had gone in about ten years ago on the border between Mourningside and Creekton.

Back in the day, Illinois law dictated that any casinos in the state had to be on water. The Seratellis' casino had cropped up to fill a void. A void in the market, a void between the two cities, a void within the criminal underworld.

A void the Seratelli family was all too happy to fill. Italians from the old country, they were just another cog in the wheel that was Creekton. With the casino, they built their own gentleman's lounges and dance clubs. They brought sophistication and class to the unsophisticated and classless.

Marcos's mother had slowly faded out of the limelight as younger and prettier girls came up. Marcos had to watch his mother take waitressing and cleaning jobs at Seratelli hotels, scrimping and saving every penny to get by.

All for the wheel of time to keep on spinning.

Marcos was glad his sister had gotten out of Creekton, happy she worked downtown for her rich father, and grateful she had a posh house on the west side—until she had been attacked. Until she'd been beaten within an inch of her life and her house had been burned down around her.

Marcos had people looking into her whereabouts, but his sister had vanished from the hospital. Momma, the nurse that had been taking care of Kara, had told him that she'd been discharged two days ago, she'd gotten in an Uber, and that was the last she'd seen her.

It was the last time Marcos had known her whereabouts. Kara wasn't answering her phone. Her house had been burned down, so she didn't go back there. He knew she wouldn't stay with her father; they didn't have that kind of relationship. It was possible that she went to stay with those guys she told him about, the three men she had mentioned that she was sleeping with. If only he'd listened to her to know anything about them... even their names.

Marcos looked up from the peeling wallpaper he had zoned out on as boots scuffling the floor got his attention.

Stone walked in with Nico "Dagger" Gage, Marcos's long-time friend and brother. Both men were dressed in Devil's Psychos cuts and had heavy rings on their fingers.

Dagger, despite his Italian heritage, was blond and blue-eyed, a handsome motherfucker with a darling smile. He was a pretty boy, but anyone that tried calling him "pretty boy" quickly learned why his nickname was Dagger.

"We got something," Stone said as they headed his way.

He watched his buddies as they took seats at the old diner table next him. "Whatcha got?" he asked, his voice raspy.

"We drove past her place. There was a navy-blue pickup in the drive, bed piled high with bags. Must be cleaning out," Dagger said.

"We saw her though," Stone added. "We rode right by as she walked out of the house. She didn't see us, and we didn't wear our cuts, but she was walking out with a bag."

Marcos took a deep breath of relief and covered his face with his hands as he tilted his head back. "Thank fuck."

"You want us to keep an eye out?" Dagger asked.

Marcos shook his head. "Nah. She's alive and doing her own thing. That's all I can hope for. She'll call if she wants to talk to me."

Both men looked resigned but nodded. They had known Kara her whole life too. They'd been Marcos's best friends since first grade. They only wanted what was best for her, and they both knew that keeping her far away from this lifestyle was the best thing for her.

No, Marcos thought, *let her live her life away from the danger that surrounds me.*

Chapter Nine

*T*HE SMELL OF SMOKE *filled her nose and choked her lungs. She couldn't breathe. Pain stabbed through her chest. She felt like she was drowning. She tried to yell for help, but it felt like she was underwater.*

Randall Diggins stalked down her basement steps toward her, gun in his hand.

She tried to scream, tried to fight back. She couldn't breathe.

He loomed closer.

"Kara!" A deep voice jolted her out of her nightmare.

A scream tore out of her throat, and she lurched upright in bed.

"Kara." The voice was softer this time. "It's me, Princess," Johnny said from her right before he reached out and turned on the bedside light.

Kara let out a shaky breath that broke on a sob, as she glanced around Johnny's bedroom. *It's not real. It's just a dream.*

"Hey, hey, baby." He wrapped his arm around her back and pulled her sideways, into his chest. "I've got you, Kara." Johnny's voice rumbled. "You're safe now."

She turned in his arms and wrapped her stitch-covered arm around him. He turned toward her and pulled her with him. He lay down slowly, pulling her with him so they were side by side. She buried her face in his chest as the sob overcame her.

He held her tightly and rubbed her back soothingly.

"You were so strong, baby. So strong. You fought him and you beat him. You saved yourself," Johnny whispered. "You didn't let him win."

She pressed herself closer to him. His chest was bare and warm. A sprinkling of chest hair tickled her face. His abs were unreal and covered in ink, disappearing under the waistband of his boxers.

She wedged her bad knee between his legs. He carefully maneuvered their bare legs, being mindful of the stitches in her knee, so they were both comfortable.

Her good hand wrapped around his back and held on tight.

He pressed a kiss to the top of her head and continued to whisper words of encouragement.

Her heart hurt. Her chest and ribs ached, and her knee throbbed. Even with the pills at dinner, she was sore.

She overdid it today at her house; she'd gone too soon. She hadn't been emotionally ready for the turmoil that would be stirred up in her mind. She imagined the nightmare tonight was probably just the beginning.

Her breathing calmed and the tears slowed.

Johnny was her fucking rock, though. He rescued her that night, and he was her salvation yesterday at the house. He saved her tonight and pulled her out of the nightmare.

She loved him. She had known for awhile. She loved him and she couldn't tell him; she wasn't ready. She was still hurting, his words had cut deep even though every damn action he'd ever done had only ever showed he cared about her.

Even that night—he had come for her. A thought struck her, and she pulled away slightly, letting the fan cool her face. "Why *were* you at my house that night?"

Johnny sighed and rolled onto his back. He kept his arm around her, but he tucked her into his side, and she rested her head on his shoulder.

She waited while he gathered his thoughts.

"I was coming to talk to you," he muttered. "Kevin and Derrick had yelled at me all day for the shit I said. They had seen things clearly, while my temper had gotten in the way. I lashed out before I could really *see* what was going on even though I could read it all over your face when you walked in the clubhouse that night." He sighed.

"You could?" She frowned.

"Yeah, babe. You looked like someone had run over your cat. You were barely holding it together."

Kara felt the tears welling in her eyes as she thought about that night and how she had forced herself to go through with breaking all of their hearts.

And for what?

In the end, it hadn't mattered. It hadn't been worth it. Her father had still tried to have her killed.

"It's part of the nickname." Johnny sighed. "I unleash mayhem when my anger gets the best of me."

Kara frowned; she didn't believe that, not entirely. He was not out of control or out of his mind with rage that night. He had chosen his words *precisely*. Meticulously. He wielded his words like a blade and stabbed them into her heart. He knew exactly which ones would inflict the most damage. And he didn't hold back.

She could still see the hate and malice in his baby-blue eyes that night. It was a look that would haunt her. It was the reason she hadn't forgiven him yet. She was too gun-shy to let him in... yet she was lying in his arms seeking comfort from him.

Tears fell down her face again.

She didn't know what to do. She wanted to talk to Kevin. Or a girlfriend.

That was it—she would call her friend Erika in the morning, get some distance from Johnny, and figure out her head. With a plan in motion, she rolled away, pulling her cast from between them and awkwardly turning to curl around the arm that had been wrapped around her back.

Johnny took the hint. He turned off the bedside lamp and rolled into her, spooning her, his bare chest against her back. In the dark, her heart pounded in her chest, his body warm around hers. She was wearing one of his T-shirts and a pair of his boxers—despite having a good chunk of her clothing now, they hadn't gotten around to washing her stuff yet.

She took a deep breath and let it out slowly, forcing herself to relax. Despite her anger and disappointment with Johnny, she was still attracted to him. He was large and warm and wrapped around her.

His cock had been rock-hard in his boxers for the last twenty minutes. For all his bad-boy personality, he was being a Boy Scout and keeping his hands to himself. She used his left arm as a pillow, and he draped his right one over her waist.

She was so small tucked into him. She loved their size difference. She loved how safe she immediately felt in his arms.

His beard scratched against her neck and shoulder as he leaned in and pressed an open-mouthed kiss to her neck.

She moaned softly and bent her neck to give him more access. When he did it again, she arched her back and ground her ass back onto his cock.

He hissed and groaned. "Baby."

She smiled in the dark. Torture came in many forms, and she was a master. She circled her hips again, and his right hand clamped down on her hip, hard. She marveled at the feeling of his tight grip. His large hand wrapped around her hip and dipped under the waistband of her boxers. "Johnny, please," she breathed out.

His hand delved deeper and she realized she hadn't shaved in a week when he slid his fingers through her folds. Thankfully she had showered at least. His finger traced along her seam, teasing her.

She rolled her hips, and he hissed and pulled away.

He turned her on her back and yanked down her boxers—his boxers. He tossed them aside and, not seeming to mind the extra hair, parted her folds with two fingers and circled her clit with his thumb. "So fucking wet for me, you dirty girl." His voice was low and gravelly in her ear, his breath hot against her skin.

She moaned again—she loved when he talked dirty to her.

"Has it been too long since this cunt had anything in it?"

She didn't know if he was being rhetorical or not, but she moaned anyway. "Please, Johnny." She begged.

"How can I deny you when you beg so prettily?" He shoved two fingers into her hole, knuckles deep.

She groaned and arched her back. "Johnny." She panted.

He slid over her, getting on his knees between her splayed legs. "Please." She begged again and wrapped her legs around his shoulders.

He gave her a cocky grin before he dove face-first for her pussy. She wrapped her thighs around his head and grabbed ahold of the hair that had grown out just enough for her to lace her fingers through.

"Fuck, yes." She panted and ground her pussy against his face. Her thighs locked around his head, and she took her fill from him.

He didn't seem to mind. He groaned against her cunt, his lips sucking hard on her clit. He slid a third finger inside her, and she shuddered. His fingers were so large, so thick.

"Johnnnnyyy." She cried out as she came, her body spasming and jacking up off the bed.

She groaned and laid back down, her hand resting on her sore rib cage as she tried to catch her breath.

Johnny pulled away from her and her legs fell open as he slowly pulled out his fingers. "Are you OK?" he asked.

Her eyes were squeezed tight as she breathed through the pain. "Yeah." She groaned. "I will be."

He sighed, but she didn't see his expression as he laid down next to her and gingerly gathered her in his arms.

Chapter Ten

KARA WOKE UP THE next morning feeling sore and groggy. She hated waking in the middle of the night—it messed with her schedule too much, and she often ended up feeling lethargic and nauseous the next day, neither of which she could afford to feel today: her appointment to get her stitches out was at noon.

She rolled over and felt for Johnny, but his side of the bed was cold. After he'd gone down on her and gotten her off, she'd tried to repay his attention, but he wouldn't have it, not after she had hurt her ribs mid-orgasm.

She hadn't argued with him, but she almost wished she had. Maybe she would have slept better after that. Instead, she slept fitfully.

She slowly rolled over to the side of the bed and sat up. Her pain levels were mildly tolerable if she were going to stay home today, but she had that appointment and would have to walk into the office.

She wondered how she was getting there. She assumed Johnny would take her, but she wished she could drive herself, but with her wrist and pain pills, she knew it would be a while before that would be possible. She'd still have to ask him where her SUV was, if it was at her house or not. Maybe he could have a prospect drop it by here if it was still in her garage.

She was dutifully ignoring the fact that she had practically moved in with him. Them? That was another question on her mind: Where the hell were her boys? She was going to give them both so much hell when they got back. After the bullshit about learning to communicate better, they had left her without a goodbye.

She shook her head. She needed to wash her face and get dressed, take some pain pills, and eat breakfast. In that order. Then she would look for Johnny and ask about her phone and laptop, her men, and her SUV.

Thirty minutes later, Kara was cleaned up and dressed and had taken her pills found something to eat in the kitchen. Johnny was nowhere to be found, though, and neither were her cell phone or laptop. Kara ventured down to the lower level of the house.

The basement was fully renovated, not that she'd expected anything else from a man who owned his own construction company. Tall ceilings, light gray walls with lots of white trim, and gray wood-grained vinyl flooring gave it a clean and modern look.

She followed the rhythmic beat of music blasting from down the hall. It steadily grew louder as she walked toward it. She passed several closed doors, only briefly wondering what was behind them. She was on a mission and wouldn't be distracted. She pushed through the double doors at the end of the hall and stumbled into a full-on gym.

Holy Life Time Fitness. Her mouth dropped open as she looked around the room. A wall of mirrors on one side made the space look bigger than it was, but it was still pretty large. On one side were two rows of cardio equipment, with two of everything, Treadmills, incumbent bikes, stationary bikes, ellipticals, and stair-steppers.

On the other side of the room were the typical weight machines you'd expect to find as well as weight benches and free weights. There was a stack of yoga mats and racks of medicine balls and kettlebells too.

She could not wait to get the all clear from her doctor and get back to working out again.

It took her a moment to locate Johnny. He was standing in front of the wall of mirrors, shirtless and sweaty, doing bicep curls. She felt her mouth drop open as she watched not only the muscles in his arms bulge but also the muscles along his back ripple with each curl.

Goddamn, he's trying to kill me. He had cut his hair too; it was freshly buzzed close to his skull, and his beard had been trimmed up again. She narrowed her eyes at him. *Funny, I just used his hair last night to grip his head, and today he cut it.* He really did know how to get under her skin.

She chose not to say anything as she leaned against the wall and watched him while she caught her breath and rested her knee. From across the room, she admired the lights shining off his glistening skin. Colorful ink ran down both arms and over his shoulders, across his chest, and down his abs and back.

The first time she had seen him shirtless she had been in awe. The man was clearly dedicated to keeping in shape. She loved how his tattoos told stories of his life in the Marines, the club, and growing up in Mourningside. She'd spent hours tracing his ink with her fingers and tongue the last time the four of them had spent a weekend in bed together.

That weekend felt like a lifetime ago.

The last couple days were the longest time she'd spent one-on-one with him ever. Their relationship was still relatively new, and they were still getting to know one another. It wasn't fair that they had the added weight of the drama that clung to them, the mistrust from both sides.

"You gonna stand there all day?" Johnny asked, not even glancing her way.

She shrugged a shoulder. "Maybe."

"Too bad. Your appointment is at noon," he told her, as if she hadn't already known.

She frowned though, wondering exactly how he knew.

"I read your discharge papers."

Her frown deepened as she stared at him. He continued to surprise her, all the fucking shit he thought of, how he took care of everything and her in the process. It blew her mind. She'd never dated someone so attentive or thoughtful before, not before Kevin or Derrick or Johnny.

"So stitches today, follow-up next Monday. Then physical therapy once you're cleared by the doc." He summarized, still not looking at her, his eyes remaining on the mirror in front of him. He didn't miss a single repetition while he spoke, alternating arms.

She nodded slowly. It sounded so simple. In reality, though, she remained in a lot of pain. She still needed to figure out how to walk and bathe and basically take care of herself on her own. As much as she wanted her independence, she would have to rely on him for a while longer.

She found that she didn't mind it so much when he wasn't being a dick. Right now, she felt raw, though, like her walls had been shattered and everything felt *too much*. She might have been able to brush off his brusque attitude on a good day, but today it hurt. Today his attitude had her feeling too much at once. She turned away from him without asking him what she'd hobbled all this way to ask.

She was halfway through the door when he called out, "Your laptop and cell phone are in the dining room."

She paused mid step. "Thank you," she called over her shoulder, not bothering to look at him.

She limped up the stairs to the living room. She didn't know how she managed it. The pain was intense when she finally reached the top. It was definitely way more effort than she should've been exerting at that point in her recovery, but she made it.

She limped into the massive great room and looked around. She hadn't yet peeked into the formal dining room—through an arched doorway to the left of the kitchen. It was as large as the rest of the space and could easily sit twelve.

On the long, dark wooden table, she found her laptop along with her cell phone. Exhausted, she took a seat and reached for her phone. She powered it on and was surprised that it started right up and had a full battery.

While she waited for her phone to load, she cracked open her laptop and fired that up as well. She saw the power cords for both were sitting on the table. Kevin and Derrick had really thought of it all when they had stopped by her place that day.

She quickly lost herself in her work emails. She was so engrossed that when her phone rang, she jumped, startled. She looked at the screen and saw her brother's name and picture. She steeled herself and slowly answered the call. "Hey, big brother." She sighed.

There was a pause on the other end. "Jesus FUCK, KARA!" he shouted in her ear.

She pulled the phone away from her ear in surprise. When she pressed it back again, she heard him beginning a tirade in Spanish. "Do you know how fucking worried I've been? *Manita*! I thought you were dead! After they called me I spent three days wondering if you were ever going to wake up! And then you just disappear?!"

"Well you weren't fucking there when I did wake up, Marcos! Where did you go? Huh, big brother? I wouldn't have even known you were there if hadn't been for Momma."

That shut him up real quick. Silence greeted her.

She rolled her eyes and continued in Spanish. "Don't fucking call me and lecture me about checking in and what not, Marcos!" she snapped. "You've been disappearing on me my whole life. Fucking hypocritical bastard."

Out of the corner of her eye she saw Johnny near the kitchen.

"I'm sorry I worried you, Marquitos. I am safe. I'm staying with my boys. I have to go. I'll talk to you later." She hung up the phone before he could say another word.

She sighed and hung her head. Fucking Marcos—everything was such a mess.

"You speak Spanish?" Johnny asked from the kitchen.

She nodded slowly. "I'm half Mexican."

She watched his eyes widen as he looked over her face. "Wow," he said. "I never would have thought."

A wry smile tugged at her lips. "My father's Scottish roots rang true for me. My brother looks more like our mother."

"That who you were on the phone with?"

She sighed and looked down at the phone in her hands. "Yeah."

"Sounded heated."

She rolled her eyes at his phishing attempts. "Usually is with Marcos." She ignored Johnny and headed for the stairs.

"I washed some of your laundry last night," he called after her. "There's a basket on my side of the bed."

"Of course there is," she muttered to herself as she headed upstairs.

The combination of his extra-thoughtful actions and aloof and brusque attitude was obnoxious. She was tired of men thinking they could take care of her while still treating her like shit. Marcos had done it all her life, her father had swooped in when she was in college and done it then, and Johnny was doing it now. Even fucking Kevin and Derrick were doing it, and they weren't even here to do anything.

Kara easily found the basket on the floor next to the bed and wondered how she had missed it when she had gotten up earlier. She found a pair of clean black yoga pants, a sports bra, and tank top in the pile of clothes. It was still probably hotter than Hades outside, considering it was early July, but she didn't see any shorts in the pile of clothes—lots of pj's and workout clothes.

She rolled her eyes, Johnny probably wanted her home and resting.

After getting dressed, she headed into the bathroom. She popped a pain pill from a bottle on the counter before she brushed her teeth, then tried to wrangle her mane of curls back into a braid with one hand.

The stitches on her left arm pulled tightly, and the cast on her right arm was a hinderance. Not to mention, she only had two fingers available to grab anything with because of said cast.

Groaning, she gave up and pulled a headband out of her toiletry bag. Once the fabric band was secured around her head and pulled her hair out of her eyes, she huffed and turned only to find Johnny standing in the doorway, watching her with an amused smirk on his lips.

She rolled her eyes and pushed past him.

"Wake up on the wrong side of the bed, Princess?" he quipped as he walked into the bathroom.

She ignored him and headed for the bed. She had an hour before they had to leave, and she was sore. Now that she had her phone, she could lay in bed and catch up on social media. She heard the shower start and looked over in time to see Johnny's naked ass as he slid his thumbs into the waistbands of his boxers and gym shorts and dropped them to the floor.

Her mouth grew dry as she watched him walk into the shower. She was still fucking frustrated over last night. He had gotten her off but refused to let her help him, and he wouldn't fuck her either. She might have come, but she was still unsatisfied.

And the more she watched his firm, plump, naked ass saunter into the shower, the more annoyed and frustrated she became.

The drive to the hospital was tense. Her doctor's office was located in a building on the main hospital campus, not quite inside the hospital but sharing the same parking lot. When they drove past the ER they had to wait while an ambulance and a minivan screeched into the emergency bay.

Kara watched quietly as a husband flew out of the driver's seat while the medical team pulled a woman on a gurney from the back of the ambulance. Her stomach rolled while watching the husband, clearly upset about his wife's injuries, walk into the ER with the medical personnel.

She had to look away as she remembered waking up confused and upset in that same emergency department. She had flailed around, inconsolable until she passed out again. Her doctor had told her that they had to sedate her to calm her down.

She shook her head. Her doctor had told her all that the following time she woke up alone in the hospital. Despite what Marcos said about waiting for her, despite Johnny's knowing damn well where she was, they'd left her alone.

Johnny pulled around the building and parked as close as he could to the medical office building.

Kara blinked away tears and got out of the truck. She didn't want him to see her crying. She didn't need his help, not if he didn't want to truly be there for her, be with her.

She heard his door close a moment after hers and rolled her eyes, ignoring him as she walked into the building. She looked up the suite number on the directory and punched the call button for the elevator.

Johnny was silent as he walked onto the elevator after her.

She ignored him.

She was called back for her appointment right on time, which she was grateful for. So many times, the doctors' offices ran behind schedule. Johnny went back into the room with her. He charmed the socks off the elderly nurse who wasn't even put off by the tattoos and leather cut.

"Alright Miss Kara." Dr. Jacobs smiled warmly as he walked into the examination room. "Let's get these stitches out." He was a middle-aged man with short light-brown hair and green eyes. She had liked him immediately the first time she'd met him.

"Sounds great." She smiled broadly.

It took Dr. Jacobs some time to remove the many stiches from her body. She had twenty alone in her left arm, where, presumably, a nail had scratched her from her tumble down the basement steps. The cut went right through her tattoo of the words *Live in the moment* just below her left inner elbow.

The tattoo wasn't completely ruined, but it was not pretty by the time Dr. Jacobs was through with it. She'd have to call her girl Slade and get something scheduled to touch it up once it was fully healed.

"Alright," Dr. Jacobs said as he worked on her knee. "Your knee is a little more swollen than it should be at this point. Have you been keeping it elevated and icing it?"

"Elevated mostly," she replied, "not iced."

"Well, start icing it. Twenty minutes at a time off and on all day, every day. Keep the knee elevated as often as you can. If you notice it swelling, it means you're doing too much and need to take it easy. This week is all about resting. Your body is still hurt," Dr. Jacobs stressed.

Kara sighed and nodded.

"Should she be walking up and down stairs?" Johnny asked, leaning forward in his chair in the corner and resting his forearms on his knees.

"Stairs are alright but not a lot if you can help it. If bedrooms are upstairs, try and stay up there and have someone bring you food. If you go downstairs, set up camp on the couch for the day. Try to avoid constantly going up and down if you can."

Kara sighed and nodded.

It was another few minutes of Dr. Jacobs removing the stitches from her knee before he moved to her ribs. "Alright, lift your shirt up and let's take a look here."

Kara winced as she pulled her tank top up, grateful for the sports bra beneath it.

"Again, you're more swollen than you should be a week out," Dr. Jacobs said, frowning as he assessed her ribs. Her skin was mottled with bruises, and the swelling had made it even more grotesque. "Your ribs are still broken. At this point they could easily puncture your lungs again. Remember the lung tissue is healing inside as well: you need to rest. It is extremely important that you don't do any jerky movements, bending and lifting, twisting of any kind while you heal. I'm ordering bed rest for the rest of the week. Stay in bed, ice the ribs and knee, and we'll reassess next week."

Kara frowned but nodded slowly.

"This is pretty swollen." Dr. Jacobs sighed as he gently prodded her ribs. "It's going to be difficult to remove the stitches."

Kara's heart pounded. She read between the lines of what he said: it would hurt to remove the stitches.

She closed her eyes and focused on her breathing as the doctor began. When she winced slightly, Johnny's hand slid into hers. She thought about dropping it, about pushing him away, but it fucking hurt, and having something to squeeze helped keep her mind off it.

"How we doing, Kara?" Dr. Jacobs asked, his voice soft and soothing.

Kara let out a shaky breath as tears slipped past her clenched eyelids.

"I know. I'm almost done. Keep breathing," Dr. Jacobs replied.

Johnny's other hand came over the top of the hand he held, and he rubbed his palm up and down her arm in a soothing motion. He was slightly behind her to make room for Dr. Jacobs, who was also on her left side. It was awkward at best, but it distracted her enough to bear the pain of the stitches being tugged through her swollen skin.

"All done." Dr. Jacobs pulled away.

Kara dropped Johnny's hand and brushed away the tears on her face.

"Alright, Kara. I know that didn't feel good. You are good to go, though. Schedule an appointment for next Monday for a follow-up. Today I want you to go home and take all of your pain pills and go to bed. Bedrest this week, OK? I'll see you next week."

She nodded, exhausted and aching, her throat thick with tears.

Dr. Jacobs left the room, and Johnny circled the table so he was in front of her.

It took her a moment to be able to sit up, but when she finally did, Johnny had to help her. "Easy," he whispered into her ear as she rested her head against his shoulder.

She bit down on her lip to keep from crying out as she groaned in pain. She had only taken one of her pain pills that morning, not all three. She hated this—she didn't want to depend on him and hated that she had to. Worst of all, she really wanted to be able to.

She choked on a sob, her fingers gripping his shirt.

"Hey." He sighed, wrapping both arms around her. "It's OK."

She hiccupped against his shoulder and shook her head. "It's not, though," she cried. "It's not OK. I'm not OK."

"I know, baby. No one is expecting you to be OK," he murmured. "I'm here for you, Kara. Lean on me, let me help you."

She shook her head again. "I don't trust you." She hiccupped again, her head still pressed against his shoulder.

He stiffened and pulled away slightly to look down at her.

She couldn't meet his gaze.

His hand cupped the side of her face, his thumb brushing over her cheekbone. "Because of what I said?" he asked slowly.

"Yes... no..." She shook her head. Finally, she looked up into his baby-blue eyes and saw his pain there, pain that echoed that in her heart. "You left me there, Johnny," she cried, her voice cracking. "You fucking pulled me out of the house and left me for the ambulance. You didn't stay. You didn't come by the hospital. You fucking left me alone! I'm always fucking alone!" she yelled at him.

He stopped moving and watched her, his eyes widening at her outburst. She was well aware that she was yelling and that they were still in the doctor's office—anyone could hear outside the door. She didn't care. She was past caring about other people's feelings.

"I'm sorry, Kara," Johnny started, his thumb resuming his rubbing of her cheek, "we had club—"

"I'm tired." She jerked her head out of his grasp, effectively cutting him off before he could blame his absence on club shit. She pushed off the medical table, ignoring him as she opened the door and walked into the hallway.

"Kara." He groaned deeply from behind her.

She shook her head and wiped her eyes as she headed toward the front desk. She needed to make her follow-up appointment and then go home and lie down. She'd pay no heed to Johnny, and the fact that she thought of his home as hers as well, until a later time.

The drive home was tense—Johnny gripped the wheel and ground his molars. She saw the muscle in his jaw clenching the whole way. She tried to ignore it, tried to ignore him, but she was hyperaware of him in the cab of the truck.

When he pulled into the driveway, neither one of them moved. "Do you really not trust me, or are you afraid that I'll hurt you?" Johnny asked, turning to face her.

"Afraid," she answered, meekly, unable to meet his gaze. She had a lifetime of being let down by the ones closest to her that only added to her mountain of insecurities.

He nodded deliberately. "I could say the same thing." He spoke softly.

"I know." Her voice was hoarse as she nodded and closed her eyes. She knew he could—she had hurt him too, had walked away from him first.

She heard his seat belt disengage before he opened the driver's side door. She watched him climb out of the truck and close the door behind him. He rounded the front of the truck and headed for her side.

She waited, frozen in her seat, for him. He opened her door and stood at eye level in front of her in the tall truck. He took off his sunglasses and tossed them on the dashboard before he gripped her chin between his thumb and forefinger and pulled her face close to his.

His baby blues were shining with emotion as they met hers.

She gasped as she got a glimpse of a rawness she doubted anyone had seen from him.

"Alright, Princess," he started, his voice raspy, "me and you are like oil and water sometimes."

She smiled weakly through her watery gaze.

"I'm sorry I left you that night. I'm sorry you were alone in the hospital. I'm sorry that I'm still learning this relationship shit and can't get my head on straight when it comes to you—I don't know which way is up or down half the time when you're around. I don't know what I'm doing most of the time..." He trailed off, shaking his head slightly.

Her tears fell freely as she listened to him spill his thoughts.

His own tears lined his eyes, and he didn't blink them back as he watched her warily. "We can fight and bicker all we like," he continued, his voice husky, "but at the end of the day, we need to be able to trust each other. We're deep into some shit here. Your dad tried to fucking kill you just to keep my dad behind bars."

She hung her head, unable to meet his gaze.

He rubbed his thumb against her cheek, and his other hand came up to cup her face, both wiping away tears. He gently lifted her face to meet his gaze. "If we can't trust each other, then we're fucked."

A smile tugged at the corner of her lips—*he has a way with words.*

"There's no point in us going any further if we can't trust each other," he continued, his own tears falling. "So tell me, Kara," he paused, brushing his thumb over her lips as both of his hands cradled her face, "what is your plan? Because I can tell you that I have *never* in my life felt this way about a woman before, nor have I ever moved one into my house before you."

Kara's eyes widened in disbelief. Her lips parted slightly as a blush warmed her cheeks. "I'm staying," she replied almost immediately. "I'm taking down my father and getting yours out of jail. And after, when all of this is over... you'll have to pack my shit yourself if you want me to leave, because I'm staying."

His lips crashed onto hers as one hand slid to the back of her head. He held her to him as their kiss turned more passionate. She closed her eyes wrapped her arms around his shoulders, and leaned into him.

He pulled away quickly, though. "I'm sorry, baby. I'm sorry I left you for the ambulance, and I'm sorry I didn't come to the hospital. I was stupi—"

She cut him off with another kiss.

"Fuck, baby." He panted when they broke apart breathless a while later. "Let's get you inside. You need to lie down."

"Johnny." She gasped. "I need you to fuck me."

"Fucking hell, Princess." He groaned against her mouth.

Chapter Eleven

KARA GIGGLED SOFTLY AS Johnny carried her in the back door of his house and set her on the kitchen counter. He didn't wait, he just pulled down her yoga pants and undies in one smooth tug and dropped them to the floor.

He devoured her mouth while he made quick work of his belt and jeans. She kept her hands on his shoulders while he took charge. She fucking loved when he was like this, fucking loved that he was finally giving in and fucking her.

He barely ran his finger over her seam—checking her arousal—before he lined himself up and slid home. "Fuck." He grunted.

She gasped and threw her head back, panting.

He snapped his hips against hers, his hands on her waist, holding her tight. She held on as he fucked her hard. "Johnny." She panted, the beginning of her orgasm coiling in her gut.

"Fuck baby." He breathed out, and his mouth latched onto her neck. She groaned when he found that sweet spot and sucked deep. He worked a thumb between them and circled her clit.

Her hands slid down his shoulders and chest and gripped the lapels of his cut, holding on tight. "Oh fuck," she cried out as her orgasm rolled over her and every nerve ending lit up in pleasure. "Johnny!"

"So fucking hot, baby." He groaned and fucked her harder.

She swiveled her hips and fucked up against him.

He groaned a moment later and spilled into her.

She rested her head against his shoulder as she wrapped her arms around him again.

"I was serious you know?" Johnny said after a beat of silence. He pulled back slightly so he could meet her gaze. "I was serious when I said I've never felt this way before about anyone."

She smiled softly and ran her hand over his jaw. "Me too, Johnny," she murmured.

He grinned devilishly and kissed her again. "Come on, Princess. Let's get you in the bath and I'll help you shave this cunt."

"You cut me and I'll cut off your balls," she warned.

Having Johnny shave her pussy had been an experience. He had been so serious and meticulous as he lathered her up and pulled the razor against her skin. Kara had sat on the bathroom counter and tried to stay still while he worked. He took his time and made sure he got every hair in every crevice.

She was soaking wet by the time he had finished. He smirked as he wiped a warm washcloth over her folds, and she moaned softly. She didn't have to ask for anything, as he got on his knees, right in the bathroom, and ate her pussy.

His tongue had done that twisting thing inside her hole that she loved so much. When she came, her cries echoing off the tile walls, he sat back on his heels and grinned wickedly.

She was lethargic and weak. Her body was still hurt and swollen, but his devilish grin only spurred her on. "Fuck me, Johnny," she whined, grabbing for him.

He sat just out of reach and it hurt to lean forward.

She tried to hook her good leg over his shoulder and pull him toward her, but he dodged out of her way. "Johnny," she whined again.

He stood up and shook his head. "No."

Her mouth dropped open in shock. She was not used to being told no.

When he turned away from her, she wanted to cry. Her emotions were all over the place, and she didn't like feeling so fragile. She watched him go over to the bathtub, though, and turn the water on. She sagged with relief when she realized what he was doing.

Once he plugged the drain and tossed in a bath bomb and a good dollop of her bubble bath, he turned back to her. "Come on, Princess. Give me a little credit here. I wouldn't leave you hanging."

"You told me no." She pouted.

He grinned and stalked toward her. "You don't hear it enough." He smirked, eyebrow cocking up.

"Neither do you, Mr. Vice President," she shot back as she crossed her arms over her chest.

He stepped between her spread thighs and rested his forehead against hers, his blue eyes boring into her own. "Oh, dollface," he hummed low, "you have no idea the wicked things I want to do to you." His voice was a sexy rasp. "We need you to get better first."

"What kind of wicked things?" she asked with a shy smile.

He nipped at her bottom lip. "The kinds of wicked things you can only dream about, my dirty girl. Come on."

"Johnny." She sighed as she put her hand in his. "Where are Kevin and Derrick? I know you said they were on a run, but what are they really doing? And don't give me 'club business.'"

Johnny frowned and stepped away from her. He ran a hand over his buzzed hair and sighed, his shoulders dropping. He met her gaze and slowly nodded. "Our brother Rachet was killed last week by a rival club. The Devil's Psychos."

Kara's eyes widened at the news. She had known a brother had been killed but not the whole story.

"He was doing a drop, out of state, with two other brothers when they were ambushed," Johnny continued. "Rachet didn't make it. It was down near Birmingham, Alabama. Kevin, Derrick, Hotrod, and Vagabond went down to bring home his body."

Tears welled up in Kara's eyes as she watched Johnny stoically tell her the truth. "As vice president, shouldn't you be there too?"

He nodded. "Yeah, I should be."

"But you're here with me?"

"I told the club you were my old lady." He moved toward her slowly.

She gasped and opened her mouth to speak.

He pressed a finger to her lips. "Shhh," he whispered. "I had to tell them my old lady was attacked in her own home because of my failure. It was the only way to explain why I was letting Rockstar and Devil kick my ass in the ring in front of every president and VP from across the country that was in town last week."

Her mouth dropped open in shock. "What?" She gasped.

He nodded slowly. "I claimed you in front of all the leaders of my club, across the country, and admitted I failed to protect you."

He wrapped his arms around her waist and pulled her against him. "I'm sorry I didn't tell—"

She cut him off with a kiss. She pressed up on her tippy-toes, grabbed the back of his neck, pulled him down to her, and kissed him fiercely. Goddamn, this man was constantly full of surprises.

When they pulled apart, breathless, he quickly shut off the bathtub before it overflowed. He peeled off his clothes and climbed in before he helped her climb over the side of the deep soaker tub.

Once they were leaned back in the deep water, her sitting between his legs, she let out a content sigh and rested her head back on his chest. His arm was wrapped around her waist, and he held her tight.

She was falling more and more in love with this man every day. She felt a small pang of remorse that she was spending all this time alone with Johnny and not the other two, but she tried not to think about it. They would be home soon, hopefully.

"Goddamn, Kara." Johnny groaned from behind her, his hands skimming over her belly and breasts, cupping them and rolling her nipples between his fingers. "You are so fucking sexy." He groaned. "Every fucking inch of you."

She felt a blush creep over her chest and neck.

"You have no idea the things you make me feel." He breathed on her neck before he pressed an open-mouthed kiss there.

He was mindful of her ribs as he traced his hands down her body again and gripped her hips. He pulled her up his body until his cock bobbed against her entrance. He slid his fingers through her folds and parted them before guiding his cock into her entrance slowly.

She laid back against his chest and moaned once he was fully seated in her.

His fingers dug into her hips and held her in place.

"Johnny." She sighed and arched against him.

"No, my little cock slut." He groaned and held her down. "You're gonna stay still and warm my cock."

"Johnny." She gasped.

"What are your safe words, Kara?" he asked, his voice deep.

She froze, her eyes shooting open. "Red for stop, yellow for slow down, and green for good," she spoke slowly.

"And where are you right now?" he asked. He gripped her jaw and tilted her head, forcing her to look at him over her shoulder.

"I—yellow, sir," she whispered, eyes lowered.

"Shhh." He hummed. His blue eyes were dark, but he didn't seem upset. It was like he was expecting this and slowly working into it. "Good. I wouldn't expect you to be OK right away. But I do expect you to be honest with me about how you feel. Can you do that for me?"

She nodded slowly. "I—I'm OK with slut," she murmured.

"Good girl." He growled and captured her lips.

Kara licked into his mouth, using her tongue to fuck into him. She clenched her pussy around him, and he groaned, his fingers digging into her hip and jaw tighter. "Naughty little slut." Johnny panted as he broke their kiss, breathless.

She loved that she was making him come undone.

He let go of her jaw and slid his hand down to her clit, toying and circling it. The other hand clamped down on her hip. He plucked and pinched her while he held her down.

"Sir, please." She moaned.

"Fucking slut." He growled and thrust up into her, hard.

She cried out, her orgasm rolling over her so quickly she hadn't expected it.

Johnny groaned into her ear as he thrust up into her again and stilled, his body shuddering beneath her.

She melted against him as she came down, fully spent and weak and unable to move.

"Fuck darlin'." He moaned as he pulled out of her. "You OK?"

"I'm great." She sighed, eyes fluttering closed. "Sore, but great."

Johnny's laugh vibrated through her back, and she smiled. He pressed a kiss to her temple and gingerly sat forward, holding her against him. "Come on, darlin'. Let's get you food, meds, and sleep. You heard the doc. Bed rest for the rest of the week."

She opened her eyes and sighed. "Alright."

An hour later she was tucked under the covers with Johnny, watching a movie with the sound low. She drifted off to sleep feeling taken care of and loved.

Most of all, she knew in her heart she loved him too.

Chapter Twelve

K ARA WOKE SLOWLY, FEELING warm and secure. She was still tucked into Johnny's side, her head on his shoulder and her leg draped over his. His arm was wrapped around her tight, but it didn't explain the heat she felt pressed against her back.

There was another leg pressed between hers, another arm draped over her waist. A tattooed hand rested on her arm that lay on Johnny's chest.

Derrick.

Her heart skipped a beat when she realized what that meant, realized he was *home*. Derrick was home, and so was Kevin.

Derrick was in bed with them.

She turned over slowly, sliding her hand over Johnny's stomach as she rolled over to face Derrick.

Derrick shifted and pulled her tighter against him. She watched his face, peaceful and serene in sleep. She grazed her fingers—the two free of the cast on her right hand—through his thick beard. It was more untamed than usual, bushier and wilder.

"Sleep, baby girl," Derrick mumbled, his eyes closed.

She frowned. "Are you OK?" she asked him softly.

He sighed and pulled her closer. "Yeah, baby girl. I'm better now."

She held him tighter and yawned. "Where's Kevin?"

"Right here, baby," Kevin mumbled from the other side of Derrick.

She smiled and reached over Derrick with her hurt hand to grab Kevin's hand and lace their fingers together.

"Sleep," Johnny grumbled as he rolled against Kara's back and curled around her.

She smiled and sighed contently, drifting off to sleep moments later.

The next time she woke, she was alone in bed. She almost wondered if she dreamed her boys returning to her, but she heard the shower running in the bathroom and could smell bacon wafting up the stairs from the open bedroom door.

Just as she was about to slide out of bed and use the bathroom, the bedroom door was pushed open wider and Kevin walked in carrying a tray of food.

His black hair was wet and freshly showered. His smile was tired, but he still looked happy to see her. "Hey, baby," he greeted.

"Morning." She smiled easily.

"I heard you got in trouble with the doctor? Ordered to bed rest?" He raised an eyebrow at her; his chocolate orbs were warm with mischief as he questioned her.

Kara rolled her eyes. "Yeah." She sighed.

Kevin set the tray on the bedside table and leveled her with a serious look. "Are you OK?"

She shrugged and looked down at her lap, where she toyed with the edge of the blanket. "Not really," she answered honestly. "I've been alone too long, and every time I let you guys in, something happens. I think we need to have a conversation about club business and what we tell each other."

Kevin nodded slowly and took a seat next to her on the bed. "In this life, the only way most relationships survive the long haul is with total disclosure." He shrugged a shoulder. "I know it's not something you wanted before..." he trailed off.

"I think things have moved past that at this point." Kara sighed, looking up at him.

Kevin nodded as the shower shut off. He took her hand in his.

"I don't like not knowing where you are, if you're safe, if you're hurt. I do better with the facts," she admitted.

The bathroom door opened a moment later, and Johnny walked out with a towel wrapped around his waist.

"We can do that." Kevin nodded, squeezing her hand.

Kara squeezed his hand and looked over Johnny's wet chest and licked her lips.

"What are we doing?" Johnny asked, a wicked grin on his face.

"Me," Kara responded immediately.

Johnny waggled his eyebrows. "Sounds perfect." He smirked.

Kevin rolled his eyes. "As much as I would love that, baby, you need to eat and take your pain pills. Lots of ice packs and resting today: tomorrow's a big day."

Johnny nodded and sighed. "He's right, baby. You need to rest."

"I've done nothing but lay in bed resting for the last day and a half. Can I at least go sit on the couch?" she grumbled. "And what's going on tomorrow?"

"Tomorrow is the funeral for Rachel," Johnny said. "You need to rest today. You'll be on your feet a lot tomorrow. As my old lady, *our* old lady," he corrected and nodded at Kevin, "you'll be expected to be there, even injured."

Kevin frowned at Johnny. "They can't expect her to ride like this." He motioned to her leg and wrist.

Johnny shook his head. "Not ride, no. You'll ride in the van with Marlie and Rachel, they're Bandit's and Welder's old ladies.

They're both pregnant. You'll probably be spending a lot of time with them tomorrow, learning the ropes of this life," Johnny explained.

She watched him warily. "What exactly does it mean to be an old lady?" she asked him.

He smirked at her and bent over in her face. "It means you're mine."

"Ours," Derrick said from the doorway of the bedroom. She hadn't heard him come up.

"To the club it means you're off-limits. You are our woman," Johnny continued, looking smug.

Kevin rolled his eyes. "It's just a title for girlfriends and wives. It means you're serious to us and not some fucking courtesan," he elaborated.

"So not just another whore?" she questioned, looking up into Johnny's blue eyes.

"Never." He growled, his hand cupping her jaw softly.

"Never." Kevin and Derrick agreed.

She nodded slowly, as much as she could with her face in Johnny's hand. "So, the four of us are doing this for real then?"

Johnny let go of her jaw, and she looked around at Kevin and Derrick.

Derrick stalked toward her and slid his hand into her curls. "Baby girl, you couldn't get rid of me if you tried. You're mine now." He claimed her lips in a molten kiss.

"Mine too." Kevin agreed and pulled her from Derrick's lips to his own.

She moaned when someone reached out and pinched her nipples. She pulled away from the three of them the best she could. "We need to have a real conversation then about expectations and boundaries. Especially since I'm pretty much living here now."

Kevin, always the reasonable one, nodded. "Yeah babe, and you need to eat. Why don't we give you some space and we can talk downstairs?"

"You mean I'm allowed out of the bedroom?" She smirked up at him.

Johnny rolled his eyes but nodded. "Yes. You can have an hour or two downstairs. Then we're tying you to this bed if we have to."

Kara grinned brightly. "Sounds great, sir."

"Fucking brat." Johnny groaned and pinched her nipple.

Once Kara had used the bathroom and eaten breakfast, they settled onto the large leather sectional in the great room. Kara snuggled under a blanket with her feet up on the ottoman, Derrick and Kevin sat on either side of her, while Johnny sat beside her feet on the ottoman, facing her.

"Alright, we need to talk about us, in terms of a relationship and our future." Kara started the conversation.

"Meaning what, exactly?" Derrick questioned, raising an eyebrow. His bright green eyes were vibrant in the morning sun shining through the wall of windows on the back side of the house.

"Well, Derrick," she drawled, "when two people are in a relationship together, they tend to share things with each other, like their daily whereabouts and work schedules, when they'll be home for dinner. Things like that."

"So, you're saying you want full disclosure?" Derrick clarified.

Kara nodded slowly, eyes darting among the three of them. "At this point, I'm compromised enough that any DA would try to prosecute, regardless of whether I actually know anything or not. I think it's better that I do know so I'll be able to properly defend myself, and you guys, should the need arise."

Kevin's eyes closed and his head tilted back in anguish and disbelief. She watched the emotions play over his face. "I never wanted this life for you." He sighed.

Kara frowned, her eyebrows furrowing. "Kevin, I would have thrown you out of my house that first night had I decided I didn't want this, didn't want you." She grabbed his hand and laced their fingers together. His eyes opened and he turned toward her as he squeezed her fingers between his.

"Full disclosure will involve you in our illegal activity," Derrick warned.

She nodded slowly. "I kinda figured as much," she admitted. "Spill it," she added with a level stare.

Derrick shook his head and smiled wryly. "Alright, baby girl. Remember, you asked for it."

When they finished detailing everything from running guns to protection details to their illegal prostitution ring, she sat in silence for a bit before her questions began.

After she was confident that their sex workers were there voluntarily and weren't being held against their will or being mistreated by the club, she simply said, "OK."

"OK?" Derrick asked, raising an eyebrow.

"OK." She nodded again. "I can deal with all that going forward. What I can't deal with is a week of radio silence. I'm not saying you tell me everything, but if this is going to be a real relationship, I expect communication to be key. Check in if you're going to be home later than you said, if shit comes up. Shit like that."

Johnny smirked.

"We can do that," Kevin answered for them, squeezing her hand.

"Real relationship?" Johnny goaded.

A smug grin spread across Kara's lips. "Yes, lover," she drawled. "You DID claim me as your old lady in front of ALL the leaders of EVERY charter of your organization."

Johnny leaned toward her, his hands resting on the couch on either side of her knees. His face was inches from hers. "You think that makes you hot shit or something?" he questioned.

Her grin widened. "I know I'm hot shit."

"Fuck yes, you are." Johnny growled and kissed her fiercely.

"Before we get sidetracked," Kevin chuckled, "maybe we need to talk about some boundaries?"

"Don't call me a whore..." she answered straightaway, though she trailed off.

Johnny's mood changed immediately, and he nodded. "Never again," he vowed.

"What about slut?" Kevin asked.

"I'm OK with slut, maybe other stuff. Just don't say *whore*," she replied.

"Safe words?" Derrick asked.

"Red for stop, yellow for slow, green for good." She smiled.

"Good girl." Kevin grinned before he grabbed her face and pulled her in for a kiss. He leaned her back against the couch while kissing her soundly.

Hands pulled down her yoga pants. "No undies, you dirty, dirty slut." Johnny growled.

"Just the way we like her, always fucking wet and ready." Derrick's deep voice rumbled next to her ear.

She yelped as she was yanked into Kevin's lap, her back to his chest. Derrick immediately slid closer, pulled her face to his, and kissed her passionately. "Tell us if we hurt you. We'll be careful of your injuries," Kevin murmured in her ear.

She nodded profusely. "Fuck me." She groaned, tossing her head back on his shoulder.

There were hands everywhere. She closed her eyes and got lost in the sensations. Derrick claimed her mouth again as he moved closer to her. She felt Johnny kneel between her legs, his hands parting her thighs wide. Cool air hit her pussy, and she groaned at how wide he opened her, hooking her knees over Kevin's. Kevin opened his legs wider, and she moaned into Derrick's mouth. She was spread open and on display.

It wasn't long before Johnny's mouth was lapping at her cunt, his breath warm and tongue hot and wet as he lapped up the center of her slit. She groaned and tried to arch into his mouth, but hands held her hips tight. Other hands palmed her breasts, massaging and kneading them through her top.

Derrick broke the kiss to help pull her tank top over her head, leaving her utterly naked in the living room before her three men. "Fucking beautiful." Derrick groaned.

Johnny's mouth latched onto her clit, and she wailed as her orgasm came out of nowhere and sent her body shuddering against him and Kevin. Derrick claimed her mouth, and her cries turned to muffled moans.

"Make her come again," Kevin said, his mouth pressed against the skin of her neck while his fingers massaged and tortured her breasts and nipples. It was a give and take, a massage and rub and then a twist and pinch.

Johnny's mouth never stopped lapping at her cunt. Two of his thick fingers slid into her pussy, and she cried out and arched against him. Kevin's hands on her tits held her firmly in place, and she groaned. She needed more.

She broke away from Derrick, panting and gasping. Johnny twisted his fingers in her cunt, and she moaned loudly. "More."

Johnny slid a third finger inside her, and she groaned. "Fuck meeee." She whined. "Please fuck me."

"Such a needy slut." Derrick chuckled.

She was shifted again as Kevin undid his belt and jeans. He stood up quickly in a show of strength, holding her hips and lifting her, forcing Johnny to take a step back. She let out a quiet squeak. Kevin stepped out of his jeans and boxers and pulled her back down onto his lap. He leaned her back against his chest and tilted her head back and kissed her, sucking her tongue into his mouth.

Kara moaned as hands started groping her again: her tits, her pussy, her hips. They spread her open and gathered her juices, coating her and Kevin's waiting cock. She was lifted again only to be lowered onto Kevin's thick cock. Moaning deeply, she dropped her head back onto his shoulder, as he slid into her wet, hot heat.

"Look at you, slut, spread out wide, pussy on display for my brothers. Anyone could walk in here and see you like this." Kevin spoke the dirty words right into her ear, his breath hot on her skin.

She panted, her back was arched, her tits heaving with every breath she took.

"God these tits are perfect." Derrick groaned before he sucked one into his mouth as he settled onto his knees before her.

Johnny's mouth came down on the other one as he kneeled on the couch beside her, and they worked her tits in synchrony. Massaging, kneading, sucking, nibbling. Fingers came down on her clit and rolled her sensitive bud between them. "Oh God." She gasped out a whine she was so close. Her eyes fell closed as she lost herself in the sensations and chased her high.

Someone's finger slid down her slit before it pressed into her hole alongside Kevin's dick. He groaned with her as she panted. "Such a good cock slut," Derrick crooned from in front of her. "I bet you can't wait to be stuffed full in this tight cunt."

Her brain felt sluggish. She heard what he was saying but didn't comprehend the full meaning. Another finger slid in her cunt next to Kevin's dick. "Oh God." She gasped and tried to arch her back.

Arms locked around her rib cage, holding her tight. Her eyes snapped open and she looked down just as Derrick slid a third finger into her cunt. "Goddamn." Kevin groaned behind her.

"Such a greedy pussy." Derrick smirked.

She wasn't given time to speak before a naked cock bobbed in her face and nudged at her lips. She barely opened before it slid into her mouth. She opened wide and sucked it in. Looking up, she saw Johnny smirk down at her from where he knelt on the couch next to them. He rested his hand on her head. "Be a good cock slut and suck."

She sucked him down and closed her eyes. Derrick removed his fingers from her cunt and she whined, missing them already. He stood up and leaned over her and Kevin, one hand bracing on the back of the couch while the other guided the head of his cock into her pussy alongside Kevin's.

She groaned and tried to arch her back as he pressed inside her, but the arm banded around her belly held her still—the twinge of pain in her ribs only added to the pleasure. Johnny's hand on her head fisted her hair and pushed her down on his dick, distracting her. He only let up when she started to gag, and then he only pulled her back briefly.

"Needy fucking skank. Fucking begging to be fucked by three men," Kevin goaded.

"Fucking hell, baby girl." Derrick hissed as he pushed into her cunt further.

"Shit." Kevin hissed too.

She tensed up as it all became too much.

"Don't tense baby," Kevin immediately said. "Shhh, just relax." His fingers slid down her belly, pressing between her and Derrick, and circled her clit. She forced herself to relax as much as she could between them with Johnny's cock down her throat.

Johnny petted her hair and kept his thrusts extremely shallow.

"Fuck, that's it." Derrick moaned. "So good, baby girl."

They worked out a rhythm and worked her body over. Fingers played with her clit and nipples, flicking and pinching and rolling her into a body-numbing orgasm. She screamed around Johnny's cock as her body shook with pleasure.

Johnny cussed a moment later before pulling out of her throat and painting her tits with his cum. "Look at this skank." Johnny growled as she was thoroughly debased, leaning back against Kevin's chest, cum dripping from her tits.

With a growl, Derrick pulled out of her cunt and came all over her tits as well; big globs of cum shot out over her body. "Fuck that's hot." Kevin groaned and shuddered behind her as he came deep inside her.

"Wanton little hussy." Derrick chuckled. "Covered in cum. Bet you're still not done yet, are you skank?"

Fingers toyed with her clit, pinching roughly. She gasped and shuddered as aftershocks from her orgasm rolled over her.

Kevin groaned as he slipped out of her cunt.

"We should keep this sloppy cunt full. Full of cock. Full of cum. That's the only way this little slut will truly be happy, huh little skank? That what you need?" Derrick kept talking as he slid his hands through the mess on her chest and abdomen. He gathered the cum sprayed there and slid it downward. "Should I put all this extra cum in your cunt? Make you hold it inside you?"

His words were sending shock wave after shock wave through her core as his fingers also worked her clit in tandem. He gathered up his and Johnny's spunk on his fingers and shoved them into her slick pussy. She cried out as he immediately circled and pressed on her G-spot and clit at the same time.

Kevin's fingers found her nipples, and she whined and tried arching her back, but again he held her in place. Her orgasm ripped through her at an alarming speed, her vision spotting as she cried out in pleasure.

"There's a good slut," Derrick murmured and kissed her gently.

That was all she knew before she let the darkness claim her and drifted off into blissful sleep.

Chapter Thirteen

MARCOS CANDELA WAS MID step, about to turn the corner into the main clubhouse barroom, when he heard the voices. "Where are we at with Mac Taylor?" the raspy voice of Devil's Psychos President Larry "The Butcher" Buckley asked.

Marcos quickly stopped out of sight to listen in. When he heard the smooth and cultured voice of that suit that sometimes lurked around—the one who looked like his suit cost more than most people made in a month—he knew he made the right decision. "I've officially taken over the case. We'll be able to get things moving here quickly. Where are you with that deal with the Snakes?"

The Snakes? He must mean those fucking Las Serpientes, the Hispanic gang that was slowly moving into Mourningside and wreaking havoc as they went. What the fuck was going on? The Psychos never did dealings with Las Serpientes. They were hated even more than the Ravager Knights were.

President Buckley was up to something dirty here. Why the *fuck* was he conspiring with this *suit* and the goddamned Las Serpientes?

"I hit a bit of a snag. I'm working on it, though. We'll get it done," Buckley promised.

Marcos narrowed his gaze as he listened. Was Buckley gonna bring this to the table for a vote? Was he making deals with Las Serpientes behind the club's back? As VP, Marcos should be in the know, but in the last several months, Buckley had grown more and more withdrawn. He'd sometimes be seen pacing the loading docks and muttering to himself when he thought no one was around.

"See to it that it happens soon. I need Mac Taylor dead. Yesterday." The smooth, cultured voice of the suit practically growled. "I didn't go through the meticulous effort of framing King Taylor for decades just for shit to get fucking screwed up by some dipshit gangbangers."

Another unusual piece. The suit was usually calm and collected, suave and gentlemanly whenever Marcos caught a glimpse of the guy. He was tall and lean, with blond hair and striking blue eyes, always cleanly put together, always in clothes that looked like they just came off a runway model.

Every time Marcos saw him he thought he looked familiar, but Marcos couldn't place him.

Buckley never shared his name, just said he was an old Marine buddy, but Marcos and his boys started referring to him as El Diablo. On the few occasions they'd actually crossed paths, the look of utter disdain the man would throw at them would send anyone running for the hills. Marcos even got a shiver down his spine at the sheer hatred in the man's gaze when he stared him down. There was something utterly wrong with the man.

"He will be." Buckley grunted. "Trust me, I want him dead just as much as you do, counselor. After all the shit he put me through overseas and my dishonorable discharge…" Butcher spat. "I'll make sure he's dead even if I end up doing it myself."

"The whole point of hiring the damn Snakes is so this doesn't fall back on either one of us, Larry," the suit snapped.

"I fucking know that, Vincent!" Buckley growled. "I just need a little more time. My VP has been sniffing around. I'll distract him and get it taken care of. You have my word, brother," Buckley vowed.

There was a slap of hands clapping together, likely to shake, before El Diablo spoke again. "I'll hold you to that, Butcher," El Diablo warned.

Chairs scuffed the floor after that. Marcos quickly walked away, as it sounded like the meeting had come to a close. He had to find Jason and Nico, tell them what he'd heard.

Not only had he gotten a first name, Vincent, but he knew the man was a lawyer and trying to frame King Taylor of the Ravager

Knights for something. And Buckley and Vincent were hoping to use Las Serpientes to kill him for them, probably while he was locked up in county.

Chapter Fourteen

T HE MORNING OF THE funeral dawned bright and early. It was overcast, but the forecast said they were safe from rain. Kara had asked if they would postpone due to rain, and Johnny had shaken his head. They would continue, rain or shine.

Kara hadn't known what to wear. While most of her fancy clothing had been ruined in the fire, she still had several bags in her car of spared clothing that needed to be dropped off at the dry cleaner's along with a load that had been at the dry cleaner's at the time of the fire. Now everything she owned was either hanging up in Johnny's large walk-in closet or in dresser drawers next to his clothing.

Johnny helped her pick out a black dress from her clothes. The guys had gone shopping for boots for her. Derrick came back with two options in two different sizes and told her to keep what fit and he would return the rest. He had a knee-high pair of high-heeled boots that were covered in zippers and studs and looked *fucking hot*. He'd also found a shorter version of them, slightly toned down but still badass, without a heel.

It turned out the high-heeled boots helped her walk with her bad knee. The black dress she wore was a simple black cotton wrap dress that hugged her curves but was still conservative enough for the office. Paired with the knee-high boots, it suddenly looked downright *indecent*, though she knew it would be alright.

She somehow managed to do her makeup herself that morning. Johnny had warned her not to cover her bruises too much, though. The club knew what had happened to her—they knew Johnny had failed to protect her from the attack. It wouldn't look right if she was too healed after not quite two weeks.

She had been healing, though. The bruising on her face was turning all the lovely colors of the rainbow. The black had turned to a bluish purple, with the edges fading to a yellowish green.

Derrick had been a doll and helped her straighten her long curly hair. Thankfully, he was used to dealing with long hair, as he had his own mane of thick locks. He did good work, and Kara was happy to be looking mostly herself once he was done.

The dress hit midthigh, and the boots ended below the knee, showing off the scarring and bruising on her knee. Add in the bright pink cast and the scar through her tattoos, and Kara looked like a badass fucked-up Barbie.

"Hot as fuck, Princess." Johnny groaned when she walked down the stairs to find them waiting in the living room for her.

Her men were all in black. Black button-down shirts, black jeans and boots, with their black leather cuts. Fresh haircuts for Kevin and Johnny, and Kevin had shaved that morning.

Kara still wasn't over the fact that Johnny had buzzed his head after she had wrapped her fingers in his locks and used them to hold his head to her cunt. She'd lay into him about it tomorrow, though. Today she would appreciate how sexy her men looked all cleaned up.

She smiled at the three of them and pressed among them. They surrounded her, pulling her against their hard bodies. She leaned back against Derrick, who immediately wrapped his arms around her waist and pressed a kiss to her neck. She reached out to grab Johnny's and Kevin's hands, holding them in hers. Kevin was gentle with her casted hand, linking their fingers together.

"You're gonna ride in the truck with Derrick. We already dropped his bike by the shop. We'll spend the day at the clubhouse," Johnny explained. "You'll spend most of the day with the women, helping out in the kitchen and organizing everything. We still have our out-of-town guests here, and even more have shown up for the funeral. Rachet was a well-known brother. He had a lot of friends, and he was murdered in cold blood by a rival gang."

"When you say, I'll be with the women most of the day..." she started, squeezing their fingers, "I don't mind that, I really don't.

But if I come up to you while you are surrounded by your brothers, strangers to me..." she trailed off, trying to choose her words wisely.

"You come up to any one of us anytime you fucking want, Princess." Johnny growled and pressed closer to her.

"You don't even have to spend the day with the women if you don't want to," Kevin added.

"You could sit on my lap all day in front of my brothers; I wouldn't mind it one bit." Derrick breathed against her neck.

She smiled slowly. "So PDA isn't too much for you big, bad bikers then?"

Kevin captured her lips before Johnny could. He pushed her back against Derrick. Derrick sucked an open-mouthed kiss into the sweet spot on the right side of her neck. When Johnny pressed against her side and sucked his own open-mouthed kiss to the left side of her neck, she moaned into Kevin's mouth.

She broke away from Kevin, breathless. She shrugged Johnny and Derrick off of her and groaned. "Fuck, don't get me all worked up before we leave."

Their laughter was deep and rumbled through her, her pussy clenching as they slowly pulled away. The heat of their hands burned into her skin. She bit back the whine in her throat and swallowed thickly. "Assholes," she snapped and walked toward the door.

Their raucous laughter trailed behind her.

When Derrick pulled the truck into the clubhouse lot behind Johnny's and Kevin's bikes, Kara sat up straighter and looked around. There were a lot of bikes and bikers around. "What do they know?" she asked, feeling anxious.

Derrick looked around and then at her. "Everything."

"What is everything, exactly?" she pressed.

"We don't have secrets in the club. Johnny stood in front of the assembly of brothers the day after you were attacked and told them that he had failed his old lady. Our old lady. That you were representing King with Danvers, and because of that, you were attacked in your home and almost killed. So because of his failure to protect you, he owed it to Kevin and I to seek our retribution."

Kara wasn't sure why she was so surprised. *Fucking Johnny, always fucking surprising me.* She chuckled softly and shook her head.

Derrick cupped her chin between his thumb and forefinger and turned her face toward him. His bright green eyes were mischievous as he pressed a kiss to her lips. "After you showed up here looking like death and half of them saw you, Johnny admitted that you were almost killed because you were helping defend Mac, that your father tried to have you killed for digging into the case. You've earned their respect," he said, nodding.

She could feel the weight of that truth in their stares as Derrick helped her climb down from the truck. She met them head-on and was surprised to find looks of respect and admiration and nods directed her way.

Johnny met her halfway, grabbed her hand in his, and led her inside. For as much of a hard-ass as he was, today he was oddly affectionate. He led her through the clubhouse to a room behind the bar where there was a full restaurant kitchen.

All eyes turned toward the door when Johnny pushed it open, and everyone slowed to a stop when they took in the vice president. "Hey everyone," Johnny greeted, looking around, his hand still in hers.

Caterers and kitchen staff, wearing T-shirts with Ravagers Knights logos on the front breast, had been busy prepping. Ovens were fired up, stovetops were fired up, and all the chefs were chopping and sautéing. It smelled delicious.

There was a group of women sitting around a table in the corner watching them intently. It was mostly to them that Johnny spoke.

"This is Kara, my old lady." He introduced her, holding up their clasped hands.

She smiled immediately as the table of women broke out into cheers. A woman older than Kara, maybe mid-fifties, stood from the table and walked toward her. Kara realized she'd seen her around before in her brief couple of visits. She was about average height with a curvy body she still squeezed into a sexy red dress and knee-high boots. She was stunning, with white-blond hair down her shoulders and striking green eyes.

"Hi, I'm Sheila, Hotrod's wife," she greeted with a welcoming smile. She held out her right hand to shake, and as Kara's right hand was in a cast, she grabbed Sheila's hand the best she could. Sheila smiled warmly and held her two free fingers, giving them a gentle squeeze. "Welcome to the old ladies' table."

Kara grinned brightly, feeling lighthearted for the first time in a while. "Thank you." She nodded. "It's good to be here."

"Come on, I'll introduce to you everyone." Sheila nodded.

"Alright." Kara agreed immediately. She glanced at Johnny a moment, and he smiled broadly.

"I'll see you in a bit," he said before he kissed her thoroughly and passionately in front of the old ladies and staff alike, then turned and headed out of the kitchen.

Kara was slightly dazed when he left, but Sheila pulled her over to the table of women. "Welcome, officially."

"Thank you." Kara grinned.

"Hi, I'm Rachel, Welder's wife," a tall brunette with pretty hazel eyes and a baby bump greeted her with a smile. She looked six or seven months along, cute and small still. She was probably around Kara's age.

Kara was introduced to the other old ladies: Sara, Gin, and Marlie. Marlie was Bandit's old lady and also pregnant and around Kara's age. She was also a paralegal at Carmichael and Associates.

"You work on ten, right? Brandon Sense's team?" Kara asked her with a smile.

Marlie smiled back tentatively and nodded. "Yeah, I uh, sorry. It's nice to officially meet you, Miss Carmichael."

"It's Kara, please," Kara replied firmly, holding Marlie's hand. "Besides, I don't think we're all that different considering the men we've chosen to be with." She nodded her head.

Marlie's smile widened and she laughed. "I just didn't want to get in trouble, you know? Big boss is here."

Kara smiled and shook her head. "After this last week, I don't even know if I still have a job, you know?"

Marlie's smile slid off her face. "Your father returned. He set up shop in your office. He made an official announcement to the board and company this morning. He said you were in a horrific car accident and would be out for several months."

"I heard this morning, when he fired my secretary." Kara sighed, squaring her shoulders.

Marlie frowned. "That's too bad. Stacy is good people."

Kara nodded wholeheartedly. "She is. I told her to do what she had to while I figure out this mess with my father."

"It's so fucked up," Rachel snapped. "Who spends forty years framing someone over some ancient history?"

"Who tries to kill their daughter after they went through the trouble of tracking them down as an adult and claiming them first?" Kara countered.

"Fucker," Sheila snapped.

"Yep," Kara agreed. "Anyway," she said, "today isn't about me or my bullshit. What are you ladies doing, and how can I help?"

They spent the next hour setting up poster boards of hundreds of photos from over the years. Rachet was an original member; he had started the Ravager Knights with Johnny's father, Mac, back in the day.

Once the poster boards were set on easels and tables around the main barroom of the clubhouse, the ladies made sure food was set for their return after the service. There would be no Mass at a church for Rachet, but they had a reverend that was a friend of the club's that would hold a service at the gravesite.

The plan was that the Ravager Knights, with all their out-of-town guests, would escort the hearse out of the compound and across town to Angelview Cemetery, on the far north side of the city. They would take the side streets, ride as a pack, and take their time. They had close to 200 bikers among the Ravager Knights, sister charters, and friends, family, and hangers-on that also rode. Kara would ride in the lead car behind the pack of bikes, with Rachel and Marlie and a prospect that had been ordered to protect the three women.

Behind them would be a lineup of cars of the people that didn't ride. There were some three hundred people who wanted to pay their respects to the fallen biker. They had a police escort and closed streets to ease their path through the city.

After, they would make the same trek back to the clubhouse, where the caterers, waitresses, and courtesans would have a large buffet set up for the several hundred guests. Johnny had mentioned they had fights scheduled for that evening in the ring, as entertainment, and lots and lots of alcohol.

It was the most beautiful and heartbreaking thing Kara had ever witnessed. It was awe-inspiring how law enforcement and criminals could work together.

Kara sat in the front with the prospect, who was driving; the girls had insisted, with her knee and being the new HBC. "HBC?" she'd questioned. Head Bitch in Charge, she had been told, because she was Johnny's old lady and he was vice president. Since King, the president, didn't have an old lady, the title fell to her.

"Congrats." Marlie smirked from the back seat. "You're queen of the bikers."

Kara's mouth had dropped open momentarily in shock before she got herself together. She was grateful when Marlie and Rachel just laughed and nodded. "Took us a while to get used to it, too—the whole biker lifestyle," Rachel said, squeezing her hand.

The service at the gravesite had been about twenty minutes. Kara stood between Johnny and Kevin. She held Johnny's hand, and Kevin wrapped his arm around her waist. Derrick stood to Kevin's right, but he had pressed a kiss to Kara's lips as he passed by.

Today, she would let them have their very public PDA because there were no photographers that would dare get close to the gravesite.

Afterward, on the long drive back to the clubhouse, the girls squealed in excitement as Kara confirmed the rumors were true: she was with all three of them. "That is so fucking hot!" Rachel shouted.

"Hot damn, boss lady!" Marlie had crooned.

Kara blushed and laughed and rolled her eyes. Something about the moment was entirely lighthearted and fun. Friendships beginning, bonds being formed during life's most somber events.

"So does that work?" Rachel asked, a sly grin on her face.

Kara looked back at her over her shoulder from the front seat. She caught a glimpse of the prospect—the same one that had been watching her house and helped Johnny move her grandmother's cedar chest—in the driver's seat and saw the blush creep up the kid's cheeks.

She smirked back at Rachel. "I mean, you have three holes for a reason."

Marlie barked a loud laugh that set Rachel and Kara giggling.

Kara turned to the prospect, who looked increasingly uncomfortable. "What's your name?" she asked.

"K-Kyle." He stuttered out his name, his knuckles white on the steering wheel.

"Kyle." She smirked, leaned toward him, and rested her hand on his arm. "I don't think I have to tell you what happens if anyone finds out about this little conversation, do I?"

He gulped audibly and she ran her finger down his arm. "N-no, ma'am," Kyle stammered out.

"Good, because we both know Johnny can be a bit..." she purposely paused, "quick tempered," she finished with a smile.

"Yes, ma'am." Kyle nodded his head vigorously.

Marlie laughed from behind her. "You already got this HBC shit in hand."

Kara laughed and shrugged.

"Anywaaaaay..." Rachel prompted.

Kara grinned and divulged a couple fun details about the number of orgasms and the attention her men had given her.

After they returned to the clubhouse, the women got to work pouring drinks and helping the staff get the food out. It took them several hours to get everyone situated, but they were just finishing up and pouring their own drinks when a woman with long black hair down to her waist stepped in front of Kara. "Kara?!" Slade Cooper shouted over the music.

She was maybe five foot five, which put her a couple inches taller than Kara. She had long black hair to her waist, striking green eyes, and was tatted and pierced *everywhere*. She was breathtakingly beautiful, modeled occasionally, and was a downright sweetheart...until you pissed her off. Then she reminded you that she was a badass who wasn't afraid to stand up for herself.

"Holy shit, Slade!" Kara shouted with a grin before she threw her arms around the woman.

Slade hugged her tightly. She was a great friend, and they hadn't seen each other in a couple months now with life being as crazy as it had been. "Fucking hell, girl. It's been too long," Slade said.

Kara nodded and pulled away. "Come on, let's get drinks and head outside."

Once they were both outside where it was a little quieter, but not by much, Slade hugged Kara again. "I heard you were hurt, but this is crazy," Slade admitted.

Kara sighed and shook her head. "It's all sorts of fucked up," she acknowledged. "Story of my life as usual though, right?"

Slade shook her head, already knowing about Kara's childhood and the stories about her father.

"What are you doing here?" Kara asked as they settled onto a picnic bench and sipped their drinks.

"I tat a lot of these guys." She motioned around the compound. "I knew Rachet. Besides paying my respects, they asked me to tattoo tonight. Lots of guys want memorial tats. So we drew up something for the night; anything past that, they'll have to schedule with me later."

Kara nodded and smiled. "Sounds like you're doing well for yourself."

"I can't complain." She smirked and leaned on the table next to Kara. "How is it that no one has signed this thing yet?!" she exclaimed and lightly patted the bright pink cast.

Kara laughed. "I've only had it a couple weeks." She shrugged. "It's just been me and Johnny for the most part since I was released Friday. Derrick and Kevin were picking up Rachet."

Slade gave her a knowing grin. "All three of 'em?" she asked.

Kara smirked devilishly and wiggled her eyebrows comically.

Slade threw her head back and laughed deeply. "Fuck yes! That's my girl!" she shouted, drawing looks.

Kara laughed along with her friend. It felt damn good to see her. It was just what she needed after all the bullshit in the last couple weeks—some much-needed girl talk. She ignored the stares around her, feeling safe at the clubhouse, and focused on one of her oldest friends.

She'd met Slade years ago; they'd grown up in the same neighborhood. While Slade had gone to public school and Kara went to the private school that Marcos and her mother had paid for, they still knew of each other.

When Kara turned eighteen and went to get her first tattoo, it had been Slade's father's shop that Kara had gone to in Creekton. Skin of a Different Breed was a well-known shop. Slade was sixteen when Kara met her, already tattooing and making a name for herself. Kara took a chance, and the rest was history. Slade had done all of her ink since then.

"Alright, girl. We need to get my pens and get this cast decorated," Slade decreed.

Kara grinned and nodded easily. "You have a blank canvas at your disposal. Do whatever you want."

"Fuck yeah!" Slade smirked and started to stand up.

"Hey, Princess." Johnny interrupted as he walked up.

Kara tilted her head up to look up at him. He leaned down and pressed a kiss to her lips. Kara smiled as he pulled away.

"Slade." Johnny nodded, a smile on his face. "You two know each other?" he asked, motioning between the two of them.

"Oh yeah." Kara chuckled. "We go way back. Slade has done all my work." Kara grinned and held up her good arm.

"That's awesome! I didn't know." Johnny laughed. "You're friends with Welder, right?"

"Yeah, I went to high school with him and Rachel." Slade grinned. "We went to the public school, while Kara was all *preppy girl, private school, Princess*." Slade joked, giving Kara a smirk.

"You know that's right." Kara smirked back, tossing her hair over her shoulder and blowing her friend a kiss.

Slade laughed and Johnny shook his head.

"I hung out with Rachel today," Kara said, bringing the conversation to a more serious note. "She's pretty cool. She was actually great today," Kara said, trying not to make it seem like she had too much fun at a funeral. She hadn't known Rachet, but Slade and Johnny had.

Slade smiled easily. "Rachel's good people. I think you guys would be great friends."

Kara grinned. "I think it's the start of a wonderful friendship!"

Slade grinned wickedly. "We are so doing a girls' night, the three of us. ASAP."

"Hell yes!" Kara shouted in agreement.

Johnny's eyes widened.

Kara smirked as Slade slapped hands with her.

Johnny groaned. "This is going to be a thing, ain't it?" he asked, motioning between the two of them. "You're gonna be trouble together, I just know it."

"Oh, absolutely!" Slade laughed and patted Johnny on the shoulder. "We wouldn't have it any other way."

Kara grinned at the two of them.

Johnny shook his head but still smiled broadly.

Slade just grinned and changed the subject. "Where do you want me to set up? I need to decorate your girl's cast, since no one has signed it yet," she drawled dramatically and pointed to Kara's arm.

Johnny's eyes widened with shock and his mouth dropped. "I didn't even think about that," he said, looking taken aback.

Kara smiled and shrugged. "I hadn't thought about it either," she said, grabbing his hand. "It's been a long week."

He leaned down and pressed a kiss to her lips. "Well, let's change that," he murmured against her lips.

She stood up and nodded, a smile on her face.

"Come on, I'll show you where you can set up," Johnny said to Slade and nodded toward the clubhouse.

Kara and Slade followed Johnny back into the chaos.

As the sun set and day gave way to night, the crowd grew livelier and rowdier. The promise of the fights in the ring was on the horizon, but Kara wasn't sure she would make it that long.

She was exhausted and hurting.

She popped her pain pills and curled up on Derrick's lap on a couch in the corner. He was talking and laughing with some of the guys while Johnny and Kevin were floating around, "making the rounds," as Derrick had called it.

Once Derrick explained that if Mac were to die today, Kevin would most likely be the next VP upon Johnny's ascension to president, Kara understood. She let them be to do their rounds of networking and curled up with Derrick when she'd had enough for the evening.

The fights were still a while off and it was relatively early, only about nine o'clock, but she was done. Exhausted and in pain, it had been the first real day out for her since she was injured, and it had taken a lot out of her. At some point one of them was going to run her home, but until then she was content to curl up on Derrick's lap.

She was dozing peacefully in Derrick's arms, floating in that halfway conscious state. She caught pieces of the conversation around her, though. "You guys just hitting that?" someone asked, and she felt Derrick tense beneath her.

His arms wrapped tighter around her, and he pressed a kiss to her temple. She let out a small sigh as her head fell into the crook of his neck and acted like she was sleeping.

"Nah." Derrick's voice rumbled low as he responded to whomever. "We're all in with this one. She's the real deal."

"Who beat her?" another male voice asked.

"A dead man." Derrick growled.

There was a pause before the guy asked, "What's that story? I've heard talk, but what happened?"

"We met her when we started doing construction on the Carmichael building downtown. Kevin's worked there for years, and they've been friendly." Derrick shrugged. "One thing led to another, and eventually the three of us got together. When King was arrested, we asked Kara for help. She's the managing partner of Carmichael and Associates. She agreed to help our lawyer with King's case. She found some shit happened between her father and King back in the day that Carmichael would kill for if it got out...Kara threatened to expose him, and he hired someone to kill her." Derrick summarized and glazed over some of the story.

She kept her breathing even as he shifted in his seat and pulled her closer to him. He straightened her bad knee out, and she almost groaned in relief.

"Who got the joy of killing the fucker that hurt her?" the guy asked, his voice husky.

Derrick chuckled. "Kara did. She managed to fight the guy off. More than twice her size, and she was half dead already, but she managed to get his gun and empty the clip in his chest. Mayhem got there just in time to pull her out of the house before it went up in flames."

"Well holy shit." The guy's voice held nothing but respect in his tone. "You got yourself a real badass there, brother."

"Yeah, Railroad, I know." Derrick laughed. "She's a firecracker. Tough as nails, not afraid to stand up to Mayhem. She's amazing."

"Good for you, brother. There's nothing greater than the love of a good woman," Railroad said softly.

The guys continued to talk, their conversation taking on a dull buzzing in the background as she was slowly lulled deeper into sleep in Derrick's arms.

Chapter Fifteen

L IFE AFTER THE FUNERAL found a steady rhythm. Most of the visiting charters went home, and Kara started physical therapy three times a week. The boys all went to work during the day, though they rotated who would take her to physical therapy since she couldn't drive.

She made her appointments earlier in the morning, so whichever of her boys took her that day would stay home and have breakfast with her before driving her. After, they made sure she was settled in on the couch with everything she'd need before they headed off to work.

By the end of the second week of rehab, a solid month since her attack, she was getting antsy. She wasn't used to sitting around so much. She was getting around better. She had officially moved into Johnny's room, unpacking all her belongings into his dressers and closet. All of her clothes had either been dry-cleaned or washed.

She'd had her girls' night with Slade and Rachel last Friday night. It was a shopping night that had turned into more drinking that shopping, but she had a good time and made a new friend in Rachel. She had been giggly and slightly drunk when she had stumbled in the front door of Johnny's house around two in the morning.

She'd sent several drunk and disorderly texts to the group chat she had with her three men throughout the night, and she'd gotten flirtier and flirtier as the night wore on. By the time she stumbled into the house, her boys had jumped her at the door and carried her up to bed... where they thoroughly enjoyed her inebriated state.

Today was Monday and time for her four-week follow-up. Johnny would be taking her before he headed into the office... his office, for Taylor Construction.

It made her realize she didn't know what to do about her own job. She hadn't talked to her father since the attack. According to Marlie, her father informed the company that she'd been in a car accident.

It was a decent enough explanation of her whereabouts, she supposed, but she still needed to figure out who in the office she could trust. Marlie had agreed to keep her updated on all things Carmichael, but she was just a paralegal on ten, not exactly someone on the executive level that could keep her up to date on her father's doings.

She was thinking about which partners she might be able to trust when her phone rang. She looked up from the book she had been reading and froze when she saw the unfamiliar number. She frowned and slowly picked up the phone. "Hello?" she answered cautiously.

"Miss Carmichael?" a male voice asked. There was a lot of commotion in the background; she could hear beeping, like a truck backing up. There were several voices yelling back and forth.

"This is she," she answered professionally.

"Hi, Miss Carmichael. This is Kenny Maris. I'm the security guard down at the Carmichael Eastlake Storage facility."

Kara froze and her mouth dropped open in shock; she had completely forgotten.

Johnny had just walked into the living room and stopped as he took in her expression. "What happened?"

"It appears we're getting a rather large delivery of boxes from the Mourningside Doc-U-Store? Are you aware of this?" Kenny continued.

"Yes, sir," Kara said quickly. "I had to call back several of our early case files. How many boxes are there?"

"Uhh. Three box trucks, ma'am," Kenny said, flummoxed.

"Alright. Will they help you unload?" Kara questioned.

"Looks that way," Kenny said. "What would you like me to do with them?"

"Unload them and put them in numerical order for me, please. Have you called anyone else about this, Kenny?" Kara pressed.

"No ma'am. The only number I have is yours, and the deliveryman said that you had ordered these yourself."

Kara tossed her head back in relief as her heart pounded in her chest. "Good man, Kenny. Good man." She breathed out a sigh.

Kenny laughed through the phone, and she could picture his jolly smile on the other end. "Alright then boss lady. I'll get these unloaded and in order for you. Anything else I can do for you?"

"No sir, I will be by this morning after an appointment to check on things myself. Thank you for the call." She smiled.

"Anytime, Miss Carmichael. It's what you pay me for, after all." Kenny chuckled.

She grinned and ended the call. She let out a shriek of excitement and ran and jumped into Johnny's arms. "Whoa there." He chuckled as he caught her. "What's going on?"

"We just got a break!" She grinned and pressed a kiss to his lips. She wrapped her legs around his waist as he held her up, her arms resting on his shoulders.

"What do you mean?" Johnny's brows pulled together in confusion.

"With your dad's case!" she explained. "I ordered back every single box of case files from our off-site storage facility. I did it weeks ago! The lady there said it would take time to organize a move that large! They're being delivered to my private storage facility as we speak. That was one of my employees calling to verify."

She was on cloud nine! They finally caught a break! She knew she would find the answers she was looking for in those boxes and anything her father might have hidden away about Case Holdings or his dirty dealings over the years.

She had a feeling the framing of Mac was just the tip of the iceberg when it came to uncovering all the bullshit her father had buried over the years.

Johnny's frown did not match her energy, though.

"What's the matter?" she asked him, looking down at his face. She rubbed her hand over his trimmed blond beard. "Aren't you happy we have a lead?"

"Of course I'm happy about that," he said hesitantly, like he was watching his words.

She narrowed her gaze on him; his baby-blue eyes were guarded. She felt her own guards slide into place and unwrapped her legs from around his waist, slowly gliding down his body. She had a feeling she would need space for the conversation that was about to go down.

It's been a while since Johnny and I argued. She squared her shoulders and waited.

"Princess, don't do that." He sighed, shaking his head.

"Don't do what?" she asked, tilting her head. Her hands came up to rest on her hips as she waited for him to explain—or rather one did; she did the best she could with the one still in a cast.

"Get defensive. I haven't even said anything yet." He groaned.

"What do you expect me to say, Johnny? I'm excited we have a lead. I'm excited that I can start digging into the case again. There's clearly *something* that my father doesn't want me to find. Why aren't you happy about this?"

Johnny ran a hand over his buzzed head and sighed. "Babe, I know you're excited, and it means the world to me that you want to help my dad. Trust me, it means everything to me." Johnny stepped toward her and rested his hands on her shoulders. "But it *fucking kills me* that something might happen to you again. I almost fucking lost you." His eyes blazed as he stared down at her with love shining through.

Her breath caught in her throat. "Johnny." She breathed out his name, reaching out to him.

He pulled her into his arms and let out a body-shuddering sob, breaking her heart. He quickly stifled it, taking deep breaths, but he held her tight. His arms were like steel bands wrapped around her body as he lifted her off the ground again. It was almost too much for her healing ribs to bear, but she was not going to let him go.

She wrapped her legs around his waist again and held him as tight as she could. She knew there was nothing she could say to ease his pain, knew there was nothing she could do to change what had happened. She'd been trying to get him to see that he hadn't failed her, but he wasn't having it.

In his mind, he should have seen something was up with her the night she broke things off with them. He should have pushed for the truth instead of pushing her away. He hadn't forgiven himself for that night—though she already had—and she wasn't sure if he ever would.

She held him and pressed kisses to his neck. She waited until his breathing was under control before she responded to him. She pulled back slightly so she could look up at him.

He avoided looking at her, but his eyes were red rimmed and still slightly damp.

She ran her hand over his beard and cupped the side of his face. "Johnny," she murmured and pressed a chaste kiss to the corner of his mouth. "Look at me," she murmured.

When his watery blue eyes finally met hers, her heart skipped a beat. Butterflies fluttered in her belly, but she felt in her soul there was no better moment than this one. She slid her casted arm around the back of his neck as gently as he could and held him in place. She spoke fiercely and deliberately. "I love you."

His eyes widened almost comically, his mouth dropping open in shock.

She smirked slightly as she saw a blush come over his cheeks.

"I don't—" He started to speak, then thought better of it. He crashed his lips down on hers a moment later. His hand curled into the hair at the back of her neck as he kissed her with everything he had.

She didn't even realize he had moved until her back hit the wall in the living room. His hands were rough as they roamed and groped her body. She moaned into his kiss as he twisted her nipple between his fingers. She broke the kiss, panting.

He kissed down her jaw as he lowered her feet to the ground and yanked her yoga pants off her. She quickly stepped out of them and her underwear before he picked her back up and slammed her back against the wall again.

His mouth worked her neck, sucking yet another hickey into her skin. She had stopped trying to hide them when out in public, and her physical therapist hadn't commented, though the woman often stared at them.

Kara groaned when his teeth sank into her flesh as he worked at the fly of his own jeans. She helped him get his pants down, and he slid the head of his cock up and down her slit, soaking up her juices before he lined himself up and rocked in hard.

She let out a loud keening wail as he slid in to the hilt. He did not slow down or stop or give her time to adjust; he started a punishing rhythm that drove her back into the wall. All she could do was hold on and enjoy the pounding. It wasn't long before she was panting and arching against him. "Fuck, fuck," she cried out before she screamed his name.

He groaned and latched onto her neck yet again before his pace picked up and he shuddered and cursed. "Fuck, Princess." He groaned and trembled against her as he spilled his load deep inside her and dropped his head to her shoulder.

They stayed still for a while, basking in the feelings of each other's arms. When he finally lifted his head and met her gaze, she could see the love pouring from his eyes before he even said anything. His fingers slid against her cheek, and she nuzzled into his hand. "I told you before, I've never felt this way about anyone ever before." He spoke softly as his fingers continued to graze her cheek. "I love you more than anything in this world, Princess."

Kara's heart soared and a wide grin spread across her cheeks. "I love you too," she replied instantly.

He grinned and kissed her deeply.

She could definitely get used to this.

Chapter Sixteen

T HE NUMBER OF BOXES that had been delivered to the Eastlake facility was unbelievable. There had to easily be a thousand boxes stacked in the large warehouse. Kenny had managed to get them all in numerical order as far as she could see. There was row after row of stacked cardboard boxes in the otherwise empty warehouse.

Eastlake was something Kara had purchased without her father's knowledge some years ago. She bought the property from a friend who needed bailing out on the loan and had vague plans of turning the space into high-end lofts, due to its location on the water, but she had never done anything with it.

Kara hired a security firm to post a couple security guards to watch the building twenty-four seven and left it unused. Until now.

After her four-week follow-up appointment, Johnny called Kevin and Derrick, and the four of them headed over to the warehouse. "Holy fuck," the guys had muttered as they walked into the large space and realized the sheer size of the task at hand.

It could take Kara *years* to find what she was looking for.

"This is insane," Kevin muttered, looking around.

Kara couldn't help but nod in agreement. There was no way she could do this alone. She immediately thought of Marlie, but she was already working full time and pregnant. She wouldn't have much time to lend, but Kara knew she would help out. She felt guilty asking, but she had no other choice. She would have to recruit help from elsewhere too and definitely call her assistant. If only she knew whom she could trust in the office. Maybe Danvers had people he could assign as well.

"What's the plan, boss lady?" Kevin asked.

She smiled and turned to him. She missed him. She missed walking through Carmichael and Associates, hoping for a glimpse of him in the hallways.

He grinned and seemed to know where her mind was. He pulled her into his arms and pressed a kiss to her lips. "The building isn't the same without your beautiful smile shining through the halls," he told her.

She kissed him deeply and wrapped her arms around his neck. She felt like she and Johnny were spending so much time together now that she barely saw Kevin and Derrick. Now that she had spilled her feelings to Johnny, she wanted to do the same with the other two, because she loved them as well.

"I think we need to do a date night. Just me and you." She purred against his lips.

"Oh yeah, babe? And what do you have planned?" Kevin hummed, his voice husky.

She chuckled softly. "I hadn't gotten that far."

"What about me, baby girl?" Derrick pressed into her back, and she sighed, leaning against him as his arms wrapped around her waist. "Do I get a date night? Johnny has been hogging you lately." He huffed.

She smirked and tilted her head toward him. Derrick took her invite to cup her jaw and kiss her deeply. "Have we fucked you yet today?" He purred against her lips.

She giggled. "It was one a.m. before we to bed last night."

"So we haven't fucked you yet, you're saying?" Derrick smirked against her lips.

"We're here for boxes." Kara rolled her eyes.

"So grab your boxes, boss lady." Kevin smirked. "We're going home."

She eagerly nodded and headed toward the first row. "Let's grab as many of the first set of boxes as we can fit in the truck."

They made quick work of loading the truck with twenty boxes of files to take home. Once Kara was positive that Johnny had secured them in a way that the tops wouldn't fly off going down the road—he put a tarp over them—she was ready to go.

"We'll meet you at home," Kevin said.

Kara nodded and walked over to her security guard. "Thanks for everything, Kenny," Kara said. "I know you have things under control here, but I'm going to be calling your office and doubling down on security now that we've got things here. I don't want you to think I don't trust you, because I do." She smiled easily. "I'm being extra cautious."

The large black man had a jovial grin and an easygoing personality. She had immediately liked him when she first met him through the private security firm he worked for. "No worries, Miss Carmichael. I already told my boss that you'd probably be calling in soon."

Kara got to work immediately on the boxes, digging through and cataloging everything she found. Everything she had looked through so far was legit, though. By the third day of digging, she was getting frustrated. She knew it would be a laborious job, but she had been hoping to find *something*.

She decided to take a risk and log into the network on her work computer. If she could search through the financials again, she could maybe pick up the trail.

She logged in and checked her emails first. She froze when she saw the email from Stephanie Stonewall of Stonewall Financials. It was sent today. Her heart leaped into her throat.

Of course! She had forgotten all about hiring her firm.

She had hired her friend Stephanie Stonewall and her company, Stonewall Financials, to do a thorough audit on their files. Kara had been so suspicious she had given Stephanie total access to their system and told her specifically not to email her and to only call her with her findings. Why had she emailed now?

Kara clicked open the email.

From: Stephanie Stonewall <S.stonewall@stonewallfinancials.com>

To: Kara Carmichael <Kcarmichael@carmichaelassociates.com>

Subject: Lunch

Hey girl,

I know life is busy. We should do lunch to catch up. It's been so long since we had a girls' night. Remember all those nights at Valle's? God those were the times! And when we'd hit up Arturo's and Karma's? Those were the best days. You should come around

> *for happy hour today if you've got time. The usual place with the*
> *old crowd. It'll be a blast from the past.*
>
> *Let me know.*
>
> *Steph*

Kara's heart hammered in her chest. There was no fucking way. Stephanie actually *found something*.

She reached for her phone and checked the time. It was going on three p.m.; happy hour would start at four. Their usual place was in Rockwell, an hour north of Mourningside depending on traffic.

She was going to be late even if she left now.

She called Kevin, knowing he was the most likely to drop everything and not ask questions. "Hey beautiful," he greeted when he answered.

"Kevin, I need you to drive me to Rockwell, like now. Can you get home fast?" she asked and headed for the stairs to change her clothes.

"On my way." He hung up, no questions asked.

God, she fucking loved that about him. No fuss with Kevin, no extra posturing or throwing his weight around. No jokes when it came down to it. If she needed him, he was there. She was realizing how each of her men was different, how she could rely on them for different things.

Kevin was her rock: always solid and always there for her.

She ran up the stairs to the master bedroom as quickly as she could with a bum knee. She was getting better. Two weeks of physical therapy, and she was walking pretty well. She still had a slight limp and some pain, but she could handle walking a hell of a lot better than she was able to before.

She was still in her pj's, so she threw on a pair of jean shorts and a bra with a black tank top, thankful that she had showered the night before with Derrick's help. He'd even put her hair up in a ponytail for her, since she still struggled to do so while down a hand. She brushed some mascara over her lashes and called it good. She still hadn't been able to master eyeliner with her left hand.

She was heading back downstairs when Kevin ran through the front door. He was dressed in a safety-green Taylor Construction T-shirt and blue jeans. "Quick, change your shirt! I'll be in the truck," she called to him as she padded down the stairs.

He flew past her up the stairs, not stopping to say hi.

She grabbed her phone and laptop off the dining room table and headed out the door, slipping her feet into flip-flops as she moved. Kara froze when she saw the fucking Taylor Construction signage on the side of the truck. It stood out like a blazing red flag. They wouldn't be able to take the work truck—it would be too obvious.

She headed back inside just as Kevin was coming through the door. "We need to take my SUV," she told him.

He nodded and held up the keys, already a step ahead of her.

She grinned brightly and headed for the garage.

"What's going on?" Kevin asked once they climbed into her MKX. It was weird sitting in the passenger seat of her own car, but she was slowly getting used to her boys driving her around.

"Six weeks ago, I hired a forensic accounting firm to look into Carmichael and Associates' accounts and Case Holdings. I wanted a thorough audit of all our records, including all of our billables to clients," Kara explained, half turning to him as he backed down the driveway.

"Six weeks ago? So before everything?" Kevin asked, slowly pulling out onto the street and putting the car in drive.

She nodded. "Yes. I ordered the audit the same time I called back all those boxes. The financial firm I hired is owned by a friend I went to college with. I told her how secretive I needed the findings to be kept, if she did in fact find anything. She emailed me today."

Kevin's eyes shot to hers, his mouth open. "Is that safe?"

Kara nodded, but Kevin had already turned back to the road. He was quickly driving them down the main street and toward the interstate. "Yes. It was a vague email about not having caught up in a while. She mentioned a bunch of shit from college and happy hour at our old hangout—she said to meet her there today."

"Hence the cloak and dagger." Kevin nodded. "Why didn't she just text your phone?"

Kara stared down at her phone in confusion. She hadn't thought about that before. When she did, her mouth dropped open in shock. She quickly powered it off and popped out the SIM card. "I, uh, I have a bad feeling, Kevin."

Kevin's hand immediately came over the center console and grabbed hers. He laced their fingers together and brought her hand up to his lips, kissing the back while he kept his eyes on the road. "I'm not going to let anything happen to you, baby."

She smiled faintly and squeezed his hand. "Know any tech geniuses?" she joked.

He smirked before his smile slid off his face and dawning realization spread over his face. "I do actually. My brother Jack."

Kara's heart sped up and a grin broke over her face. "Would he help?"

"Absolutely," Kevin said vehemently.

The hole-in-the-wall bar that they pulled up to in the small town of Rockwell, Illinois, didn't even have a sign out front with the name of the place. The locals knew it as The Squirrel Cage.

Kara walked in with a smile on her face. She left her cell phone and laptop in the car, hidden under the seat. Kevin had made sure to park in clear view of the window. He followed her in, his hand sliding to her lower back as they walked through the door.

She found Stephanie sitting in the back corner booth, their usual spot. Her back was to the door. Kara and Kevin slid into the booth across from her, and she startled.

"Girl, never leave your back to the door like that," Kara scolded.

Stephanie jumped and looked up from her phone, clearly caught unaware. "Shit girl." She hissed, clutching her chest. Her auburn hair was pulled back in a tight ponytail that accented her high cheekbones. Her bangs were cut on an angle and swept away from her face. She wore a pair of rectangular black-rimmed glasses that framed her face and gave her a sexy-librarian vibe. Her green eyes were vibrant and full of energy as she swept her startled gaze over Kara and Kevin.

Kara raised her eyebrow at her pointedly.

"Who's this?" Stephanie asked, a slow grin pulling across her lips as she took in Kevin.

Kara laughed and shook her head. "Stephanie, meet Kevin Adams, my boyfriend," she introduced. "Kevin, meet Stephanie Stonewall, one of my very dear friends from our days at Northern Illinois University."

"Before she went all Ivy League on me." Stephanie smirked.

Kara grinned and shrugged.

Kevin shook Stephanie's hand and smiled. "Always nice to meet Kara's friends."

"And meeting one of Kara's boyfriends is not something I do often," Stephanie said, giving Kara a pointed look.

Kara laughed and shook her head. "So anyway..." she drawled. "What did you find?"

Stephanie immediately turned serious and got down to business. She pulled out a flash drive and handed it to Kara. "It's so much worse than what you were thinking. Case Holdings has pocketed *millions* over the years from every single client your dad has ever touched along with several other senior partners at the firm."

"Ken Laraway?" Kara asked, pocketing the drive quickly in her jean shorts.

"Ken Laraway." Stephanie nodded. "Jim Briggs. Reid James. Janet Walter. Just to name a few."

Kara's heart plummeted into her belly. "The entire senior partner staff?"

Stephanie shrugged. "It's hard to know if they even knew what they were doing, you know? Case Holdings is listed as a research firm. There were tons of miscellaneous charges for *research*. It's possible that they didn't know, not really," Stephanie suggested.

Kara was doubtful. She wouldn't hold her breath on a couple of those names. Ken Laraway definitely knew. Jim Briggs was another of her father's old friends. Reid James and Janet Walter, she honestly couldn't say one way or the other. They weren't close with her father, but they had good professional relationships with him.

"There's a folder on the drive with my breakdowns and thoughts on my findings. I detail what I found and what it COULD mean, without my knowing the truth from these people." Stephanie sighed.

Kara nodded thoughtfully. She knew her friend was thorough, hence why she hired her in the first place. "Why didn't you call me?" Kara asked after a beat of silence.

Stephanie looked around the bar. "I, uh, didn't know if you were being watched... you know? With a lot of those implicated being your father's employees, I wasn't sure if your phone was safe."

Kara nodded slowly. "I had the same thought on the way over here. I'm going to reach out to someone I trust to make sure my devices are safe," she admitted.

"Good idea—you can never be too careful. You should also look into a private security firm for the time being. I suggest not going anywhere alone," Stephanie said, looking sheepish. "Not that your man can't protect you, just you can never be too cautious."

Kara nodded slowly and eyed her friend for a moment. Something was definitely off about her. She wasn't quite... herself. Kara couldn't put her finger on just what the issue was.

When Stephanie looked around the bar again, Kara followed her gaze to a large man in the opposite corner dressed in a pressed suit. He was large and intimidating, hints of tattoos on his neck peeking out above the collar. He made a show of watching the TV hanging over the bar. The game was on, but his eyes barely moved, like he was watching them out of the corner of his eye.

"Who's the thug?" Kevin said, having seen him too.

Stephanie whipped around and looked at Kevin with a startled expression.

"Steph, are you OK?" Kara asked, feeling uneasy.

Stephanie forced a smile to her face and nodded, almost too quickly. "Yeah, yeah. Great," she stammered.

Kara shot her a look. *I don't buy your shit.*

Stephanie sighed. "The thug is with me. He is private security."

Kara's mouth dropped open in shock. "Stephanie, what's going on?"

Stephanie shook her head. "It's not what you're thinking. It's just my job, you know? I'm hired to dig. I dig into all sorts of unsavory people hiding money. It can be dangerous at times." She shrugged a shoulder. "It has nothing to do with your case. I've had a couple run-ins the last several months."

Kara was dumbfounded. "Stephanie." She sighed.

Stephanie plastered a bright grin on her face. "Don't worry about it, babe. I've got it under control. Just want you to make sure you stay safe too." Stephanie nodded at her cast.

Kara bit her lip and nodded. "I've got things under control too." She sighed and leaned sideways into Kevin.

Stephanie smiled genuinely and nodded. "After all this blows over, let's do a real girls' night. Get some of the old gang back together?"

Kara relaxed and grinned. "Absolutely."

Stephanie also relaxed and nodded. "We're gonna be OK."

Kara nodded back even though she still felt uneasy. There was something more going on with her friend, but Stephanie didn't want to share, so Kara would have to let her handle it on her own.

Chapter Seventeen

Aﬁer Kara and Kevin left Stephanie at The Squirrel Cage, Kara called Johnny from Kevin's phone and asked him if Derrick was nearby. Once she had both men on the phone, she explained to them what she was up to. "Kevin said his brother could help. I need to make sure my laptop and cell phone don't have any kind of tracking software that my father is using."

"You think he'd go that far?" Johnny asked.

"I honestly don't know anymore. I feel like I don't know anything about my father." She sighed, feeling upset and overwhelmed.

Kevin reached out and squeezed her thigh, leaving his hand there as he drove her car.

"OK, baby girl," Derrick said. "You do what you gotta do. You guys headed there now?"

"Yeah," Kara answered. "We're already up this way. We're just gonna head into the city and meet Jack at his place."

"Alright, Princess," Johnny agreed. "You guys stay safe."

"We will. I'll check in later," Kara agreed before she hung up. It felt weird not ending the call with *I love you*, but she hadn't told Derrick or Kevin yet, and she wanted to tell them herself. Johnny agreed and understood. It was only a matter of time before she told them—the feelings were already there, just not spoken aloud.

The drive from Rockwell into Chicago was slow. It was a Wednesday evening, though, and they were going against traffic, trying to get into the city, while everyone else was trying to get out of it, so it wasn't horrible.

Kara's brows rose as they pulled into the driveway of Jack Adams's home in Buena Park on the north side of Chicago. It was practically a mansion in the city. Scratch that, she thought, there was no practically—it WAS a mansion.

Kevin pulled her MKX into the long brick driveway that ran down the side of the house. "This is unreal," Kara muttered, looking around the neighborhood as they got out of her car. The house had to sit on four or five lots.

Kevin chuckled. "Be sure to tell Jack how much you love it. It's his pride and joy. It apparently was built by some prominent architect back in the day for some jewelry tycoon or something," he explained.

Kara could only nod in awe as she looked around; it was spectacular. "It's fucking amazing," she murmured.

"Well thank you, I think so as well." A male voice spoke from behind her as she was taking in the backyard.

Kara turned to find a man in a suit who looked very much like Kevin. A little younger and leaner, but still very much as attractive and with the same black hair and brown eyes. There was no mistaking they were related; he had a mischievous air about him and the smirk to match.

"Hey brother." Kevin grinned and walked up to his younger brother, hugging him tight.

"Hey bro." Jack grinned as he hugged him back, no posturing between the two of them, just a good hug between brothers.

When they pulled apart, Kevin held his hand out to Kara. She went to him, and Jack grinned and held his left hand out to her, having noticed the cast. "Jack Adams," Jack introduced himself.

"Kara Carmichael." Kara grinned, shaking his hand firmly. She was a lawyer after all.

"As in the pretentious law firm?" Jack asked, raising an eyebrow as he dropped her hand.

"The one and only." Kara nodded as Kevin wrapped an arm around her waist and tucked her against his side.

Jack chuckled and scratched an eyebrow with his middle finger, his watch glinting in the light coming from the coach light on the garage. "And you need my help?" he questioned.

Kara nodded, but Kevin spoke before she could. "Can we talk inside?" he asked his brother.

"Of course." Jack nodded.

Kara quickly opened the back door of her MKX and pulled the laptop and cell phone out from under the seat. She handed them over to Jack and followed him inside.

Jack switched to business mode almost immediately, and it would have been comical had she not been nervous as to what he was going to find on her devices.

He led them through the back door and into an amazing chef's kitchen. She barely got a chance to look around before he headed through a door and down the steps to the basement.

Kevin grabbed her hand and followed after his brother.

Hours later, Kara sighed. She was exhausted. Jack was still going through everything. He had quickly found that she had been right to be concerned. There was tracking and listening software on both her phone and laptop.

He had removed them for her, then he started digging into her devices to see what else he might find. He discovered a hidden app that recorded all of her written messages as well. After he had declared her devices clean, he still recommended getting new ones just to be safe.

She had agreed, defeated, and curled up on the leather couch in his office while he started digging into her father. She gave him the flash drive from Stephanie and her father's personal information... and dig in he had.

Now she was exhausted; it was going on midnight, and Jack didn't look like he was quitting anytime soon. When she yawned midquestion, Jack glanced at the time and frowned. "Why don't you guys head upstairs and take the guest room?" he suggested to his brother. "I'll probably be awhile yet."

Kevin looked down at Kara, who was resting her head on his shoulder. "Yeah, that sounds good."

They got up slowly and Kevin led her up the basement stairs and through the kitchen to the main stairwell in the massive front foyer. The house was a spectacular architectural design with mahogany trim everywhere. She was too tired to truly appreciate it. By the time they got up to the second floor and into the guest room she was half asleep on her feet.

Kevin helped her out of her shorts and bra, leaving her in a tank top and undies, before he tucked her under the covers. "I'm gonna hang out with my brother for a bit longer. I'll be back in a bit," he said before he leaned down to kiss her.

"Mmm." She hummed against his lips, eyes already closed.

He chuckled as he pulled away. He was pretty sure she passed out before he even left the room.

She woke to the sun peeking through the slats of the blinds. Kevin was curled around her back, snoring softly in her ear. She relished the feel of him behind her and enjoyed the quiet moment. It wasn't often she got alone time with him anymore. She missed him—missed what they started together, though she was grateful for Johnny and Derrick.

She was going to have to make an effort, after all of this was behind her, to make time to spend with each of her boys alone. One-on-one time was important too.

She stretched languidly and rolled over to wrap her arms around him. He shifted in his sleep, pulling her closer, but otherwise remained dead to the world.

She brushed her fingers over his sleeping face and along the stubble growing in on his jaw. He was so fucking hot, even in his sleep. She brushed her thumb over his lips and gasped when he sucked it into his mouth.

His eyes snapped open, and she was caught off guard by the intensity in his almost black eyes. She pulled her thumb out of his mouth as his hand slid up her back and wrapped around the nape of her neck.

He pulled her in closer and captured her mouth in a fiery kiss. She hummed into his mouth as he rolled them so he was perched over her, his hips nestled between her spread legs. Only the thin scrap of her panties separated them.

She smirked when she realized that he'd come to bed naked. He was so fucking warm against her, his whole body an inferno that set her heart racing. She looped her arms around his neck as she shifted her hips wider and bent her knees, getting comfortable.

Kevin smirked and pulled away from the kiss when she hummed and thrust her hips up against his. "Did you want something, naughty girl?" His voice was husky from sleep. He nipped her jaw and she hissed when he licked it better.

She circled her hips up toward his again, grinding on his cock. Her hand slid down the golden skin of his toned back, reveling in the expanse of hard muscle and smooth skin. "Please, sir." She moaned and nipped at his chin.

He lowered more of his weight down on top of her, and she sighed. "My dirty little slut hasn't asked properly yet," he crooned into her ear. His breath was hot and sent shivers down her spine.

"Please, sir." She moaned, her voice breathless. She pressed an open-mouthed kiss to his neck, just below his ear. "Please fuck me. Please use me like a dirty slut."

Kevin didn't say another word; he reached between them and ripped her panties off her body.

She let out a quiet yip as the fabric tore, grateful they weren't any of her lace or silk pairs. She generally hated those panty-ripping romance novels solely on the fact that sexy underwear was expensive! And to ruin a matching set for sex? Fuck those guys.

She couldn't blame him, though. It was fucking hot when he lost control and took charge of her. She loved every minute of it.

He didn't give her time to get ready either. He glided the head of his cock through her folds, slicking himself with her juices before he slid in deep. He didn't give her a moment of reprieve as he set a punishing pace.

She wrapped her legs around his trim hips and met his thrusts with her own.

He pulled her arms from around his neck and placed them above her head. He laced his fingers through hers—careful of her cast—and held her in place as she groaned and arched against him. His lips found that spot on her neck and latched on.

She gave another breathy moan as she tried to free her wrists only for him to tighten his hold. "Kevin." She panted softly.

He kissed his way up her neck and nipped at her jaw again. "What did you call me, slut?" He growled into her ear, his hips halting.

She cried out, frustrated. "Please, sir. I'm sorry, sir." She begged. "Can I come please, sir?"

Kevin pulled away and hovered above her; his brown eyes were intense as he stared down at her. His gaze roamed over her face, studying her. "I don't know, slut," he muttered. "You've been working a little too hard lately, haven't been resting enough. Do you think you deserve it?" he questioned; a sparkle glinted in his eyes.

Her eyes narrowed on their own, almost pulling her out of the scene to snap at him about all the hard work she was putting in on Mac's case, until his other hand wrapped around her neck loosely. She swallowed thickly as her mind blanked out once again.

"Think carefully about that answer, pet," he murmured, a smirk tugging at his lips. His hand squeezed her throat gently.

Her lips parted as she gasped, eyes wide. "I will try to relax more." She panted.

His eyes narrowed and his hand tightened on her throat. "Try again." He snapped his hips against hers.

Her eyes fluttered closed as a moan ripped from her throat. "I will." She moaned. "I WILL relax more," she vowed.

"You can do better than that, slut." Kevin's voice was so deep and commanding butterflies fluttered through her belly as her spine tingled and her core clenched around him. He was torturing her.

"Please, sir!" she cried out, trying to arch against him.

He held her firmly in place by her throat and wrists.

"I PROMISE, SIR!" she shouted, eyes snapping open. She met his gaze with her own. "I promise I will relax more! Please, sir, please can I come?"

He finally smiled and started thrusting his hips again before he finally said, "Come for me, my love."

She came instantly, crying out his name. Her eyes shuttered closed as her orgasm rocked over her. Her back arched and her fingernails dug into his hands.

He pounded into her, riding out her orgasm, prolonging it. "Fuck." He growled before his lips captured hers and stole her breath away. His body shuddered as his own orgasm ripped through him.

When she broke the kiss, breathless, he settled down on top of her, resting on his forearms so as not to crush her. His forehead grazed hers. When she opened her eyes, she found him staring down at her, a soft smile on his face.

She grinned and lifted her chin, pressing a kiss to his lips. Their kiss turned more passionate as he opened for her and slid his tongue against hers. They made out in the afterglow, neither of them willing to let the other go.

When they finally pulled apart, they didn't go far. He hovered over her, looking down at her with eyes full of emotion. She gasped, sliding a hand over his cheek—she felt it too, the absolute surety of the moment. She smiled, sensing what he was about to say. She waited a moment and said it with him.

"I love you."

His voice was husky and deep; hers was light and breathy, but they spoke those three little words at the same time.

He grinned and kissed her again.

Tears leaked out of the corners of her eyes as she kissed him back with all she had. She had loved him for a while. Johnny and Derrick too. Just two down and one to go. She would need to get some one-on-one time with Derrick in the next couple of days.

Maybe Kevin was right—she had been working a lot lately. She could use some time to rest with her boys. She wanted to tell Derrick how she felt, sooner rather than later.

When Kara and Kevin finally headed down to the main floor, they found Jack in the kitchen. He was sitting at the impressive island, drinking coffee, and staring out the back windows into the large backyard that *did not* look like it belonged in the middle of Chicago.

Jack looked over and smiled when they walked in. "Morning," he greeted.

Kara smiled warmly as Kevin headed toward the coffee machine. "Morning. Were you up late?" she asked.

Jack took another sip of his coffee. "I haven't gone to bed yet." He chuckled.

Kara's mouth dropped open. "No." She sighed. "You should have gone to sleep. It could have waited, really."

Jack held up his hands and shook his head. "Don't worry about it. I wanted to help. Usually, I'm the one asking Kevin for help with something. It's nice to be able to do something in return."

Kevin smirked. "You could learn to swing a hammer yourself, then you wouldn't need me so often."

Jack rolled his eyes. "I need to be able to hack into the government at the drop of a dime, not break a hand or finger because I screwed something up."

Kevin chuckled and handed Kara a mug of coffee, fixed just the way she liked it with a dash of creamer. "So did you find anything?" Kevin asked his brother.

"Found lots. Can't prove much, though. I dug for it illegally," Jack said.

Kara frowned but nodded. "And what did you find?"

"Case Holdings is a shell company, obviously. They've been listed as a research firm on all of the billable hours your father and the other senior partners have ever billed."

Kara nodded. "Right. Stephanie said that much yesterday."

Jack nodded and continued. "Yes, and I'm sure from your own digging you discovered you couldn't find much on Case Holdings.

Any income they receive goes into an account owned by Candy Creek Inc., yet another shell company."

Kara's eyebrows creased as they pulled together. "I did manage to get that far when I was searching through our records. I even went as far as looking into Candy Creek through public records. Candy Creek was established as a business by the Candle-Carla Trust. So, I started digging into the Candle-Carla Trust, and the only trustee I was able to find was Candy Creek Inc."

Jack smiled broadly. "You did good work. I was able to dig deeper for you, though. The Candle-Carla Trust is registered to a law firm in the Cayman Islands: Carlita Associates."

Kara gasped and her heart plummeted to her stomach.

"Kara?" Kevin moved in closer, wrapping his arm around her.

"Say that again." Kara gasped, eyes wide.

Jack looked concerned. "Carlita Associates is the name of the law firm in the Cayman Islands. Candle-Carla Trust is registered to Carlita Associates and owns Candy Creek Inc. Candy Creek is just another shell company being used to funnel the money from Case Holdings out of the US. Jack spelled it out for her.

Kara had to sit down. She stumbled toward the barstool at the island and flopped down. Her heart was pounding. She couldn't breathe. How was it that after all this time she hadn't seen it? Never put two and two together?

"Kara?" Kevin asked, concerned.

"My mother's name was Carlita Candela. She was a single mother trying her hardest to raise two kids in Creekton," Kara explained slowly.

The truth dawned on Kevin's face as he slowly sat down at the island with her and Jack.

"She tried her best, but life was hard with two kids. Marcos protected me from a lot growing up, but it wasn't a secret that mom was stripper. Things were always tight growing up, single mom, two kids, same ole story." She shrugged. "She went by the name Candy at night. During the day, she cleaned houses. The women in the neighborhood often called her Candle because she always had a smile on her face." Kara smiled sadly, remembering her mother. "She could light up a room just by walking in and smiling.

"I don't know how I missed this." Kara shook her head. "My dad has been retired for the last year, traveling he's said, but I tracked his flight info —he's mostly only ever gone to the Caribbean. How could I not have looked deeper?"

"Hey, don't beat yourself up," Jack said. "He did a really good job hiding his tracks, an amazing job actually. I'm just better, and a lot of that was made easier by the report from Stonewall Financials. Your friend definitely gave us both a head start. You had the right idea hiring a forensic accountant."

Kara nodded slowly. Her head was swimming.

"So now what?" Kevin asked.

"Now you have to build your case," Jack said, looking at Kara. "Everything Stephanie gave you is legal. You can connect the dots to your father with that, then dig into Carlita Associates in the Caymans. You should be able to find the legal registration for it. Might have to take a flight, but you should be able to find it."

She nodded slowly. "I can do that, build my case and present it to the DA."

Kevin smiled grimly. "You going to be OK?" he asked.

Kara shrugged and shook her head. "I'm not sure."

"Let me know if I can help with anything else. I already gave Kevin a new laptop and cell phone. They'll be the most secure things you can use."

Kara forced a smile on her face. "Thank you, Jack, and thank you for digging. Seriously, I appreciate the help."

"Anytime, Kara. It was nice to meet Kevin's girl for a change." Jack smiled.

Kevin groaned loudly and Kara laughed.

"I'm sure Mom will love to meet her," Jack continued.

"Don't you dare." Kevin groaned.

Jack grinned. "I have to now that I've met her. What else am I going to tell Mom about during our weekly call? All I do is work, and I get tired of her ragging on me to settle down. Let's get her focused on you for a change."

"I hear the same shit you do, so don't act like you're the only one who hears about it!" Kevin snapped good-naturedly.

Kara let out a breath she didn't realize she was holding and smiled easily as she let herself relax. It was nice to be around siblings who genuinely loved each other and had friendly banter. It made her miss her brother. Despite their last argument, he was still her big brother, and she still loved him.

She made a note to herself to call him when they got back home.

Chapter Eighteen

JOHNNY STALKED AROUND THE outside of the clubhouse, feeling uneasy. He didn't like that Kara and Kevin had gone into the city alone last night without backup. He understood the why of it, but it still didn't sit right with him. He knew Kevin could handle protecting her, and his brother Jack was good people, but Johnny still felt uneasy with her gone.

He missed her.

He didn't get to talk to her before she went to sleep. Kevin called him and Derrick after she passed out to let them know that they would be spending the night at his brother's place.

That was last night. Now it was going on early morning and the clubhouse was mostly quiet, but there were always those that didn't sleep through the night. Johnny was one of them. Derrick too, apparently.

"What's going on with you, man?" Derrick asked, falling into step with Johnny as he made his rounds around the perimeter of the compound. It was still dark, not yet four a.m., and Johnny kept to the shadows, not feeling up to company.

Devil wasn't one to heed Johnny's moods, though. He often stuck like glue whenever Johnny sank into darkness.

Johnny glanced at him and shook his head. "Something's off." He grumbled, not sure how to explain what he was feeling. It was a gut instinct that he didn't understand himself, but he'd learned to trust it over the years.

Derrick's green eyes missed nothing, though. "You miss her." He smirked.

Johnny rolled his eyes. "Of course I miss her. I fucking love her. I want her home already."

Derrick let out a bark of laughter, throwing his head back. "I never thought I'd see the day that you, Mayhem, would fall in love!"

Johnny rolled his eyes and his shoulders, uncomfortable. This is why he kept his mouth shut about shit, fucking loudmouths like Devil. "And you haven't?" he shot back, raising an eyebrow at Derrick.

Devil grinned broadly, his sparkling white teeth shining in the dim lighting. "Oh absolutely, but I'm not afraid of love. I'm just waiting for her to get there herself."

Johnny smiled, thinking of their girl. "I don't think you'll have to wait much longer, brother."

Devil grinned wickedly. "Oh, trust me, I know she's itching to say it. She's been dancing around it for weeks. It's become a game now to see how long I can keep her on the edge of her seat."

Johnny chuckled and shook his head. Fucking Devil, always a jokester.

Commotion at the gate had Johnny whipping around to see what was going on. The sounds of flesh hitting flesh rang across the compound lot. "Fuck." Johnny swore when he saw his guys crowded around a lone man on the ground.

He took off at a jog with Devil on his heels only to skid to a halt when he saw a Devil's Psycho on the ground in the circle of Ravager Knights. The Knights were stomping the holy hell out of the Psycho.

Rage rolled over Johnny. "Enough," he shouted to his men when it was clear the Psycho was unconscious. The Knights immediately fell back, and Johnny moved in, able to get a better look at the half dead man on the ground.

Johnny didn't recognize him. "Who is he?"

"Not sure, but we caught him climbing boxes on the other side of the fence and looking over. Taking pictures by the looks of it," Hotrod answered.

Bandit was looking through pictures on the phone. "We might be able to get something off this." He waved the phone once.

Johnny nodded. "Do it."

Bandit didn't need to be told twice. He headed for the clubhouse, and Johnny saw Marlie meet him halfway. Johnny looked away when the couple briefly kissed, need panging in his chest as he realized Devil had been correct: he was missing Kara something fierce.

"He alive?" Johnny asked, nodding down at the unconscious piece of shit littering the pavement.

"Barely," Mammoth answered, his voice a deep gravelly growl.

"Send him back to the Psychos," Johnny ordered. "Staple a message to his fucking chest if you have to, but tell the fucking Devil's Psychos if they send another spy, they're asking for a fucking war." Johnny's anger rolled off him. His men nodded around him, not a word of dissent spoken. "Clear out the fucking fence line," Johnny snapped. "Standing on fucking boxes, looking over? Fucking amateur bullshit," he grumbled and walked away.

Devil followed him. "Dude, this is getting out of hand with the Psychos. Between this shit and the trade routes being disrupted..." He shook his head.

"I know we voted with all our charters to move the trade routes to avoid fucking conflict," Devil growled, "but at this point they're fucking asking for it, and we're running with our tails tucked between our goddamned legs."

Johnny's eyes narrowed on his buddy. It wasn't like him to question his decisions as club vice president. "You want to start a war? Now?" Johnny growled, turning to face his buddy head-on.

Devil shook his head. "If King—"

"King's locked up, brother." Johnny growled, getting in Devil's face. "My dad is locked up." Johnny heaved a deep breath. "And *that* is exactly *why* we can't afford to kick shit off with the Psychos. They have more men on the inside. We want our president back alive and whole." Johnny growled again. "We gotta play the fucking long game."

Devil paused and eyed Johnny before picking his words carefully. "I get that, man, I do, but they know we're vulnerable. They know King is our weakness, and they are using him to press us even further."

Johnny sighed and turned away from his friend and brother. He ran a hand over his buzzed head and tried to think this through. He knew Devil was right, but the club voted across all the fucking charters—it was bigger than just them. They voted to move the trade routes to keep the peace for now, for King's sake.

Johnny had never been as grateful for the club as he had after that vote. His own fucking father's life was on the line while he was in the county jail awaiting trial. Johnny was mostly on his own in a gang war that had hard lines and even harder enemies.

The Psychos had so many of their own inside it was unreal. King was outnumbered. And that's not even mentioning whatever deal they had with the Italians and the fucking *snakes* that were Las Serpientes.

Johnny was grateful they had managed to get his dad some protection from the Bratva. The fact that they'd worked well with Tarazov's crew over the years was something that had put Johnny's mind at ease. With the Russians at their backs and the trade routes shifted to avoid conflict for the time being, it bought them some time to get his father out of county.

Kara was confident that she had what she needed to put her own father behind bars. Between her and Danvers, they would succeed, and Mac Taylor would be home soon. Johnny just had to have faith.

"Look, brother," Johnny sighed, "I'm trying here," he admitted because it was Derrick, his brother.

Derrick immediately cooled off and sighed. He too, turned away. Tensions were high, there was no doubt about it. Everyone was getting worked up over the Psychos' bullshit. Kara's being targeted by her father and her recovery were only two more things that weighed them down.

"I know, man." Derrick sighed. "Shit." He shook his head.

Johnny nodded, already knowing how fucked up everything had gotten.

God, they needed a fucking break already.

Chapter Nineteen

MARCOS WAS SLEEPING WHEN the racket kicked off in the clubhouse, shouting and banging pulling him from a deep sleep. There was a bang on his dorm door before it was opened and Stone pushed his head inside. "Yo, Marc, we've got problems. Nickle was just delivered, beat half to death by the fucking Knights."

"Fuck." Marcos cursed and rolled out of bed; a quick glance at the clock showed it was going on six a.m.

He pulled on his clothes from the night before. Everything was right where he left it. He didn't usually stay at the clubhouse, as he had his own apartment, so he didn't keep much in his dorm.

He slipped his feet into his boots and pulled his cut on as he walked out of his room and into the long hallway that led to the main barroom. Angry male voices grew louder the closer he got. "Those fucking Knights ravaged Nickle!" someone shouted.

Marcos stormed into the fray of angry brothers to see what the hell was going on. Nickle was laid out on the floor with everyone crowded around. Marcos couldn't see shit. "Move," he snapped at the crowd of men.

They parted and Marcos could see firsthand how beat-to-hell Nickle was. "Motherfucker." He growled, his blood boiling as he took him in. "They stapled—"

"Next spy gets the bag," Stone read from next to Marcos.

"Why the FUCK was he spying on the Knights?" Marcos growled, turning to the room.

"I sent him." The raspy voice of President Buckley answered from the back of the room as he hobbled into view.

Marcos was quick to school his expression before he turned to face his president.

Buckley was an aging man of sixty-five. His health and body were deteriorating faster than he'd like; some days Marcos thought his mind wasn't far behind. Buckley was hunched over from a bad back and should be on oxygen but often went without it because, in his mind, it "made him look weak." His full head of hair was white, along with his beard, and his hair was pulled back into a greasy ponytail. His face was wrinkled and leathery from age and too much sun over the years.

Buckley shuffled in, looking older than shit, a scowl on his face when he saw the state of his spy. "He dead?" he asked, voice hard and emotionless.

"No, sir," Russel, a prospect, answered.

Buckley grunted and moved closer, taking in the sign stapled to Nickle's chest.

Marcos caught Stone's and Dagger's eyes as they moved closer to the scene. "Why was he spying on the Knights?" Dagger asked Buckley.

Stone caught Marcos's eye and shook his head subtly. He hadn't heard about it either, apparently.

"Because I fucking sent him," Buckley barked. He turned his acidic gaze on Nic and glared.

Nic wasn't intimidated in the least and raised an eyebrow in return. "Did I miss a vote?" Nic asked, sarcastically. "Since when are you giving out orders to spy on a rival without a vote?"

Buckley squared his shoulders and turned fully on Nic, clearly ready to fight. "I'm the president of this club. I did what I thought was best!" Buckley growled.

"By sending a brother on a fucking suicide mission without backup?" Stone snapped back.

Grumbles of agreement went around the room.

"You should have at least had a conversation with me," Marcos spoke up. "I'm the fucking VP of this club."

Buckley rounded on him, fire in his eyes.

Marcos could see the mania in those angry gray eyes, the glint of something unhinged and not right staring back at him.

Buckley had always been a little over-the-top when it came to taking risks. He lived by the seat of his pants most days, but he could usually be made to see reason when something wasn't safe for a brother or good for the club.

Sending a lone man to spy on the Ravager Knights?

They're lucky Nickle was even breathing. He might not be for much longer either, unless they got him to a hospital or called a doctor. "He needs a hospital," Marcos stated and stared down Buckley.

"Call the doc, Griff," Buckley snapped.

Marcos shook his head. "He needs a fucking hospital or he's going to die on the fucking floor."

"Then it's his own damn fault for getting caught." Buckley growled.

Disbelief rolled over Marcos.

"You motherfucker," Stone snapped, stepping forward. "He's our goddamned brother, and you sent him to his death, for what?"

Buckley ignored him and turned away, heading for the door.

Marcos growled with anger, but Nico got in his way, putting his hands on Marcos's chest.

"Let him go," Nico muttered, face close to Marcos's. He looked serious, and there was a knowing glint in his eye.

Marcos glared at his friend, too angry to see reason.

Nico shook his head, subtly. There was more at play here.

Marcos took the hint, but anger boiled through his veins. He couldn't sit back and do nothing while their president walked away from a dying brother.

Marcos ripped out of Nico's grip and pushed past him. "I'll bring the truck around. We're taking him to Mourningside General," Marcos snapped and headed for the door.

Chapter Twenty

WHEN KARA AND KEVIN got back from Chicago, she went straight to work on the case. She set up shop in the dining room of Johnny's house and dug in hard. The new information from both Stephanie and Jack had her able to build a solid case for the district attorney.

The DA was a friend of hers, of sorts, someone she had worked with many times over the years. Kara might not have been a criminal defense attorney, but every now and then her corporate clients needed things handled delicately, so to speak.

She dug into the flash drive that Stephanie had handed over and pored over file after file. She grabbed a fresh legal pad and started her notes, logging every single thing she could find to present to the DA with the evidence to back it up.

She needed to build an airtight case to not only lock up her father for all his lies over the years but to also get Mac out of Mourningside County Jail and back home with his son.

Kara was so lost in work she didn't notice when the sky grew dark or the guys started cooking dinner in the kitchen. She didn't even see Johnny and Derrick until they were standing right in front of—and behind—her, pulling her away from the table.

"Shit." She jumped, startled when lips landed on her neck and hands slid around her waist.

Derrick pulled her back against his firm body. His beard tickled her neck as he sucked on her sweet spot, further bruising her already marked skin.

Johnny's hands immediately cupped her breasts as he stepped into her body and pushed her back against Derrick's solid mass.

"Ohhh." She groaned, realizing what was happening as Johnny smirked down at her and squeezed her breasts tightly as he kneaded them like dough.

Her mouth dropped open in a low groan, and he didn't waste any time, claiming her mouth with his own. His tongue slid against hers, toying with her, thrusting into her. Her eyes closed as she slid her hands up his chest and around his neck, being careful with her cast.

Derrick's hands smoothed down her stomach and quickly undid the button of her jean shorts, the same ones she had worn to

Jack's house the day before. She hadn't bothered to change when she'd gotten home. She'd been too busy getting to work.

"No fucking panties." Derrick growled against her ear when he found nothing but bare skin beneath the denim.

"Kev stole 'em." She panted, breaking apart from Johnny, breathless.

"Such a dirty slut." Johnny growled before his teeth bit down on the side of her neck.

She cried out, throwing her head back against Derrick's chest.

"I say she should never be allowed panties again." Derrick growled too before he spanked her ass roughly.

She whimpered and writhed between them. They were both pressed so tightly against her she could barely move. She didn't want to be anywhere else.

Derrick pulled her tank top over her head while Johnny slid his hands around her back and quickly undid her bra. He pulled it from her body in a quick yank that left her panting.

"Such a wanton little thing," Johnny grumbled, his voice deep.

Kara moaned and reached for him, needing more.

He resisted her, though, when she tried to pull him back down to her mouth.

"Johnnyyy." She whined, digging her nails into his shoulders.

He chuckled deeply, his blue eyes blazing with lust and something darker, *something* sinister. "Oh no, my wanton little slut," he crooned, wrapping his hand around her throat. He applied enough pressure to make her swallow thickly. "You will be playing by *my rules* tonight."

Her heart rate sped up. There was a dangerous air behind that sinister smirk he now sported. She nodded mutely, her head barely able to move while he squeezed her throat.

"What do you say, slut?" Johnny demanded, his eyes darkening.

"Yes, sir," she answered immediately.

"Good girl." His hand squeezed a little tighter around her throat.

She gasped out a breath as Derrick slid his fingers through her folds from behind. Two fingers shoved into her pussy, and she moaned softly. She loved when they took charge of her like this, loved when she was able to shut off her lawyer brain, all the over-thinking she constantly did, and let them guide her to orgasm.

"What are your safe words, Kara?" Johnny asked, his hand still tight around her neck.

"Red for stop, yellow to slow down, and green for good," she said, her voice raspy.

"Where are you now?" he asked, raising an eyebrow.

"Green, sir. So greeeeen." She keened as Derrick twisted his fingers and added a third digit inside her.

Derrick chuckled softly in her ear before his lips sucked her earlobe between his teeth.

Kara's eyes fell closed as she lost herself in the sensation of Derrick's fingers working her core. She barely paid attention to Johnny as he shifted against her until there was a bite of pain on her nipple. Her eyes flew open, and she cried out. She tried to grab for it before she realized what was happening.

Johnny and Derrick were quicker than her, though. Johnny grabbed her left hand while Derrick grabbed her right arm above the cast so as not to hurt her. Johnny let go of her neck, and she took a deep gulping breath as she looked down at her breast. There was a rubber tipped clamp tightened on her nipple, and Johnny wasted little time attaching a second nipple clamp to her other breast.

Kara looked down at herself in shock. There were alligator nipple clamps attached to each tit, with black rubber protective pieces softening the blow to her skin, but the pressure was still tight and pinching. There was a silver chain that connected the two clamps and led down to a chain dangling from Johnny's fist, and she couldn't see what was in his hand. "Safe word," Derrick demanded against her neck.

"Green." She moaned, leaning her weight back against him. She tilted her head up to meet Johnny's penetrating stare.

"You were a bad little slut while you were away." Johnny spoke, his voice low.

Her mouth dropped open in shock. She had left to find out more on the case. His father's case.

"You broke one of your own rules." Derrick growled in her ear, his fingers still pumping in and out of her soaked core.

"What?" she mumbled. Her eyebrows furrowed in confusion. Her mouth was parted as she panted. Her nipples were on fire already. Her pussy throbbed, and despite Derrick's ministrations, she was still too far away from tipping over the brink.

"You didn't keep us updated while you were away," Johnny added, his voice deep and serious.

"I called you guys when we were headed to Jack's." She gasped, trying to twist between them. They each still held one of her arms. "You both were OK with it." She tried to reason.

"You did call," Johnny nodded, "but did you think to tell us you were spending the night?"

Kara gasped as realization dawned on her. She had fallen asleep and didn't even text the group chat. She hadn't even thought of it this morning when she woke up. Granted, she assumed Kevin had told them, but she should have asked him about it. She hadn't considered keeping them updated.

She would have been pissed had they not at least texted her after everything they had been through, everything they still had going on. Radio silence was *not* safe. "Johnny, Derrick, I'm so sorry. I thought—"

Johnny tsked and shook his head.

Derrick withdrew his fingers from her pussy.

She whined.

"Our little slut is going to learn a lesson tonight," Johnny said roughly and opened his hand, revealing a third clamp.

It took her a moment to realize what she was seeing. A third clamp that was attached to the chain between her breasts. It dangled down from her nipples toward her... Her eyes widened in shock as her mouth dropped open. "No," she snapped.

"No?" Johnny growled. "You don't tell me no, slut." He grabbed her hips and hauled her up, letting go of her hand.

She fought against him, kicking out. "NO!" she shouted.

"Safe word or bust," Derrick said in her ear behind her. His hand released her arm and fisted in her hair. He wrenched her head to the side so he could see her face. The concern in his green eyes warmed her heart, but she wasn't in the mood for gentle.

"No." She growled again and kicked at Johnny.

The smack to her inner thigh had her shouting out as Derrick slapped her ass at the same time. "Fucking brat." One of them growled.

Her surprise at the dual smacks gave them the brief respite they needed to get her back under control. Derrick wrapped his hand around her throat, and she could feel her own juices coating his fingers as he gripped her neck. His other hand was still in her hair.

Derrick had her neck and head thoroughly immobilized.

Together, Johnny and Derrick maneuvered her to the table and roughly slammed her on top of all her papers. Johnny pried her legs open and stepped between them before she could close them. All the writhing and jostling only added to the orgasm rising within her. She panted as much as she could with Derrick's heavy grip on her throat.

She squeezed her eyes shut and cried out, arching her back as the clamp closed down on her swollen clit. "Fuck!" She swore, her voice hoarse.

Johnny didn't give her any reprieve either. He shoved two fingers into her pussy immediately, and she gasped. He pumped her hard, each thrust of his fingers jostling her whole body. Her tits bounced, making the clamps swing and pull on her tortured nipples.

"Goddamn, she's a dirty slut," she heard Kevin say. He sounded so far away. Sounds were muffled. All she could hear was the roaring in her ears and her labored breathing.

"Fucking tramp is what she is." Derrick growled before his mouth descended on the top of her breast and he sucked and bit her skin just above her nipple.

Johnny curled his fingers inside her cunt as he added a third digit. He rubbed the pads of his fingers into that spongy spot behind her clit. He stroked and circled and pressed into her G-spot until she was arching her back off the table, trying to escape his torture.

Tears ran down the sides of her face as she started to sob.

A hand came down hard on her belly and pushed her down onto the table. Fully immobilized, it was the last straw.

The orgasm that ripped out of her body had her vision turning white behind her eyelids as stars exploded. She screamed as her body shook and she creamed all over herself and the table.

"Oh fuck, yessss." Someone gasped in awe. She didn't know who, didn't care. She was lost in the waves of pleasure as her orgasm continued to shake her body. She felt like she was floating above the table. Her eyelids were heavy, as were her limbs. Her whole body tingled; she was hot and feverish.

She must have passed out, because when she came to, she was groggy and confused. Something smelled delicious, though. *Dinner.* Someone shifted her, and she felt a cock slide in her pussy, thrusting slowly. Hands wandered her bare skin, skimming over her belly and breasts. Her clit and nipples were aching, almost burning with the pain she felt in her most sensitive places.

She slowly opened her eyes and realized she was sitting in the kitchen, at the table in the breakfast nook. She was sitting on Derrick's lap, by the looks of it, and Kevin and Johnny were across the table from her. She was leaned back against Derrick's shirt-clad chest, her head tilted back on his shoulder.

She gasped as she realized what was happening.

He's fucking me while they're eating dinner.

Steaming plates of pot roast and roasted veggies were set before them. Kara moaned softly and turned her head into the crook of Derrick's neck. His beard brushed her face, and she buried her face in further.

"Rise and shine, baby girl." Derrick chuckled as his hands squeezed her hips and pulled her down further on his cock.

She gasped as her over sensitized and swollen pussy slid further down his rock-hard cock. "Derrick." She moaned, trying to swivel her hips only to realize there was still a clamp on her clit. The chain slid over her belly and hung from her nipples, where the clamps were also still firmly in place.

Her pussy clenched down on Derrick's cock as she realized what had happened after she'd passed out—how they were using her body. She moaned and tried to swivel her hips again.

Derrick landed a soft smack to her outer thigh. "Uh-uh, baby girl." He grumbled in her ear. "You'll sit still and warm my cock while I eat dinner. You won't move and you won't come," Derrick instructed, his voice deep in her ear.

She gasped again.

Her eyes landed on Johnny and Kevin; both men were watching her like she was the most beautiful thing in the world and they'd never see her again.

"What do you say, slut?" Kevin asked, raising an eyebrow at her.

"Yes, sir," she replied, her voice hoarse and low. She cleared her throat, feeling extremely parched.

"Drink," Derrick commanded, pressing a cool glass of water into her hand.

Her hand was surprisingly steady as she lifted the glass to her lips and took a deep gulp. It felt like heaven on her scorched throat.

"Easy," Johnny murmured, his blue eyes blazing.

Kara lowered the glass to the table and sighed. "Am I allowed to eat?" she asked softly.

"Absolutely," Derrick replied, handing her a second fork. "Dig in." He motioned to the heaping pile of food stacked on his plate, clearly enough for the two of them to share.

She smiled and loaded her fork... only to quickly realized how hard it was to lean forward and eat over the plate while she was impaled on Derrick's cock. His hand gripped her hip as he thrust forward, spearing her further.

She moaned around a forkful of food.

Kevin and Johnny were watching her with devilish grins on their faces.

They were all evil, sadistic bastards, each and every one of them. She would hate them if she didn't love them all so much.

Dinner continued on at a torturous pace. She ate slowly, and Derrick fucked her slowly, with punching thrusts that stole her breath away.

"Eat your food, slut," Johnny ordered when she stopped chewing the meat in her mouth.

She hadn't realized she'd closed her eyes until she had to open them to meet Johnny's gaze across the table. The smirk on his devilishly handsome face was sinful. His blue eyes were dark with desire, and there was not a hint of wiggle room or slack in those beautiful blue eyes.

She was condemned to her fate.

She quickly swallowed her food and then took a drink of water. She would have to eat quickly or she would never survive the meal.

When dinner was finally finished and the table was clear of dishes, Derrick stood up, with her still impaled on his cock, and bent her over the kitchen table. She had to brace her arms on the table so her clamped nipples wouldn't brush the surface.

"Better hold on, my lovely little tramp. You're in for a wild ride." Derrick growled into her ear before he snapped his hips against hers.

"Oh fuck," she cried out. She tried to brace her forearms on the table and use the friction against the wooden top to keep herself in place, but her cast got in the way, making her slip.

"Stay down," he snapped. Then his heavy hand came down between her shoulder blades and shoved her upper body against the smooth wood table.

Her clamped nipples crashed onto the cool wood. She hissed as pain lanced through her tits and sent a roaring current straight to her cunt.

Derrick's hand held her in place while he set a brutal pace with his hips.

Her world dimmed around her, narrowed down to just the two of them. Just the slapping of his hips against hers. The sounds of skin on skin, smacking with the sheer force of his thrusts. The squelching sound of her pussy quivering around his cock. Her labored pants as he pushed the breath from her lungs with every slam of his hips.

She cried out loudly as her orgasm tore through her. Her walls clamped down on his cock, milking him. Her body shuddered beneath his, and still Derrick continued to pound her pussy.

"Such a good cock slut." Derrick growled into her ear. He leaned over her and wrapped a hand around her jaw. He pulled her head back and devoured her mouth with his. His tongue twisted against hers and claimed every bit for himself.

She was limp and helpless as she gave herself over to him completely. When her body collapsed bonelessly against the table, Derrick broke the kiss. "Good girl," he murmured before he pressed a chaste kiss to the tip of her nose.

A moment later he pulled out and came with a loud groan, shooting his load all over her back and ass.

She could only lay there, cum splattering against her skin.

She heard the click of a camera shutter and groaned.

"Such a dirty, messy slut." Kevin's voice came from behind her.

A faint smile pulled at her lips, and she struggled to stand up. "Can you clean me up?" she asked softly. Her voice was hoarse, her throat dry.

"Nuh-uh." Kevin chuckled darkly, still behind her. She heard another click.

Her heart fluttered. She trusted him. She knew he would never ever show anyone those photos, but she couldn't deny the fear and heat that flared through her at the thought of her boys having dirty pictures of her to look at later.

"Please, sir." She tried again.

Johnny's deep rumbling voice answered from her right. "No slut. Tonight, you will stay as dirty as we please until *we decide* you can clean up."

Kara turned her head to the right to see him with a length of rope in his hands. Her eyes widened. They had talked about bondage before. Her guys generally restrained her hands and arms during sex with their own hands. They hadn't brought toys into this yet, not like they were tonight. The clamps, the chain between them. Now the rope.

She opened her mouth to say something—she wasn't sure what—when Johnny cut her off. "Safe word, slut."

She blinked at him in confusion, her mind slow to follow.

"Kara," he stated, a small frown on his face.

"Green. So green," she replied.

He eyed her carefully. "And to stop?" he asked, stepping toward her.

She frowned. *Why is he making me think right now?* "Red," she mumbled and finally pushed off the table.

She stood up, feeling Derrick's cum sliding down her back.

Johnny stalked toward her. The length of rope dangled from his hand.

She stood frozen, like a deer in the headlights, watching her predator stalk toward her. Because that's exactly what Johnny was: a predator. The deadliest kind. His blue eyes narrowed as he stood before her.

"Any last words before we stuff that mouth full for the rest of the night?" His voice was deep and commanding.

She licked her lips slowly, enjoying the fact that his intense gaze traced the slow, sensual swipe of her tongue.

She startled when a hand slid down her back, through the mess of cum on her skin. She looked over her shoulder to see Kevin there, a wicked grin on his lips. His deep brown eyes sparkled with mischief. "You going to behave tonight, or are we going to have to punish you?" He quirked an eyebrow at her.

Her mouth dropped open in shock. She couldn't answer that, didn't even know *how* to answer that. They made punishment sound so delicious. Would it really even be punishment if she enjoyed every moment of it?

Kevin's wicked grin turned into a devious smirk. "Cat got your tongue, pretty girl?" His hand slid through the slick of Derrick's cum and rubbed it down toward her ass. He circled it around her puckered hole and she groaned. Her nerve endings were on fire.

"Kevin," she mumbled.

"Sir," he corrected before landing a quick smack to her backside.

It took her a moment to register the sting from his quick love tap. Heat flared along her ass and in her belly. "I'll behave, sir," she answered.

"Good girl." He chuckled deeply, his voice smooth like caramel. His breath was hot against her ear as his fingers resumed their circling of her hole. He dragged his fingers through Derrick's cum again before he pressed inside.

A low moan escaped her lips, and she tilted her head back to rest against his shoulder. He sucked an open-mouthed kiss into her neck before he pushed her upper body back down on the table.

She barely got her arms up in time to prevent her aching nipples from hitting the table again.

While Kevin worked his fingers into her ass, his foot came between hers and kicked her legs further apart, widening her stance. "Arms behind your back, tramp," Kevin ordered.

Her breath caught in her throat. *What?* Her mind raced as she thought about her poor tortured nipples. She wouldn't be able to brace against the table.

His hand slid around her belly and found the chain connecting her nipples to her clit. There was a gentle tug that made her cry out. Her body instinctively followed the tugging down to the table to relieve the pressure.

She quickly complied with his order and put her arms behind her back.

"Like this," he said before he quickly arranged her the way he wanted. He positioned her arms so she held the opposite elbow with each hand, as much as she could with a cast on her right wrist, at least. He added a second finger in her ass before she heard the telltale sound of a lube bottle lid popping open.

She committed to the position, letting her weight rest fully on the table, her nipples crushed against the cool wood. She turned her head to the side and rested it against the table. She watched Kevin move to the left while someone came up on his right.

"Do you know what Shibari is, my pretty little slut?" Johnny asked, his voice thick with desire.

She gasped and went preternaturally still as a smooth rope slid up her legs and over her backside.

"Words, Kara." Johnny reminded her softly.

"Japanese rope bondage," she replied, her voice breathy.

"That's right. And your safe word?" Johnny asked again.

She loved that he checked in with her throughout the scene. Loved that with each new element he added he made sure she was still on board with it. "I'm green, my love. So green," she replied, a broad smile on her face.

Johnny leaned over her and pressed a kiss to her lips. "We're going to blindfold you and tie you up. We're going to use you in every single hole you have and leave you filthy like the dirty little slut you are. The world will know you belong to us."

Her heart raced with every single word Johnny's deep, gravelly voice spoke and the way he growled them at her while he roughly squeezed her jaw. Butterflies danced in her belly.

She'd never in a million years let a man speak to her the way she allowed her three men to. She didn't even allow them to speak to her that way outside of a scene, but she couldn't deny how much she loved these scenes. She loved how much it turned her on when they called her *slut*, when they used her body like the whore she was.

Oddly, the word didn't bother her in her head.

Derrick walked toward her, fully dressed, dangling a blindfold from his fingers.

Johnny's hands were gentle on her arms as he wound the rope around her limbs, being extra careful not to squeeze her arms together too tightly due to the hard cast.

Kevin resumed stretching her ass open, his fingers sliding inside her again.

Derrick smirked down at her before he slid the red velvet blindfold over her head. The fabric was soft against her face, but the thick material made it so zero light penetrated beneath it.

She gasped. Her heart raced. Her senses came alive, sensations magnified.

Johnny stopped moving behind her, his ropework complete. She could feel it wrapped around her wrists and forearms, snaking around her upper arms and biceps before crisscrossing over her bare back. She tried to move, fidgeted.

She was stuck. Completely immobile.

Her heart rate sped up and her breaths came out in short, gasping pants.

"Safe word, slut," Derrick said, his voice sounding far away.

"Yellow," she murmured, frowning slightly. She wasn't sure if that was how she really felt. She trusted her men explicitly. She wasn't in danger. She wasn't in pain. Was she just scared?

"You're doing so well," Johnny murmured in her ear before he pressed a kiss to her temple. "Breathe."

She shook a deep breath through her nose and slowly let it out.

"Good girl," Johnny praised.

She felt herself calm and slowly relax again.

Kevin twisted his fingers in her ass as he slid a finger into her cunt. "Perhaps she needs a job to do," Kevin drawled as fingers circled her clamped clit.

She gasped and bucked against his hand. She cried out when she was suddenly lifted by hands on her waist. The loss of Kevin's fingers left her feeling empty.

An arm scooped up under her knees while the other wound around her back. She was lifted into strong arms and cradled against a muscular chest. She recognized Johnny by his scent—leather and mint.

She snuggled into his chest as he carried her up the stairs. She assumed they'd entered the master bedroom when she was finally set down on her side. She stayed where she was while her men moved around the room.

She listened to the sounds of fabric sliding and falling to the floor; presumably all three of her men were getting undressed. A smile pulled across her lips as she imagined what they saw: her, naked, blindfolded, and tied up on the bed, nipples and clit still clamped, cum dried to her back and ass.

She didn't even know why she had thought yellow earlier. "So green," she murmured, mostly to herself.

The answering chuckle from her men, though, sent the butterflies in her belly soaring. She was in heaven and loved every minute of it.

"Enjoying yourself, little slut?" Derrick asked.

She grinned in return. "Yes, sir."

"Good girl," he answered, the smile evident in his voice. "Now make yourself useful." His fingers fisted tightly in her hair, and he yanked her up and onto her knees at the edge of the bed.

Derrick stood in front of her, his cock pressing against her lips. She opened her mouth quickly and sucked him down. His grunt was music to her ears as he pulled on her jaw, roughly, and yanked her forward, forcing her to swallow him down. With her arms tied behind her back, pushing her breasts out and making her posture straighter, the chain connecting her nipples to her clit pulled taut and tugged relentlessly on her aching bits.

Derrick gripped her face roughly as he fucked her mouth with enough force that she was left breathless. All she could do was focus on her breathing and let him use her as he wanted. The bed dipped behind her before fingers found her cunt again and more lube was squeezed onto her puckered hole. Then rough hands grabbed her ass and pulled the globes apart, thumbs sliding into her puckered hole and stretching her open before a thick cock slid in.

She moaned around Derrick's cock. The dick in her ass slid in slowly but didn't stop until it was fully seated inside her. The man behind her roughly pulled her upright with the rope laced around her arms, yanking her off Derrick's cock.

She groaned as her tortured nipples and clit were pulled by the chain. She gasped and panted, head leaning back against the man behind her.

The bed dipped as her men shifted around her. Hands on her hips lifted her up while keeping her impaled on the cock in her ass. "Tuck your knees up," Johnny demanded from in front of her. His rough hands grabbed her legs, helping her bend her knees and lift her legs.

The bed shifted again "I'm going to lower you down onto Johnny." Kevin's voice was deep and gruff in her ear. "Easy with the knees."

Hands grabbed her thighs gently. "Come 'ere," Johnny murmured as he guided her legs down and around his hips as Kevin set her down. Once she was straddling Johnny's wide body, his grip on her thighs tightened.

Together, Johnny and Kevin lifted her enough to slide her down onto Johnny's thick cock. "Fuck." She groaned as he bottomed out.

"So fucking hot, baby girl," Derrick said from a few feet away. She again heard a camera shutter.

Johnny's hand wrapped around the back of her neck and pulled her down against his chest, the clamps crushed between them. She groaned but wasn't given a moment of reprieve before Derrick shoved his cock between her lips again.

She moaned around his cock and got lost in the fucking, the slapping of skin on skin. Her mind emptied of everything but the feeling of her men using her body so thoroughly. Her orgasm crashed over her and she moaned loudly. Her body shuddered as she gasped around the dick in her mouth.

As she came down from her high, the cock in her mouth was removed and she was hauled upright by the ropes binding her arms. "Such a good slut," Johnny ground out as his cock slammed up into her cunt.

Pain exploded across her body as the nipple clamps were removed without warning. She arched her back, throwing her head back against Kevin's shoulder and crying out in pain as blood rushed back into her battered nipples. Kevin's hand slid up her sides and cupped her sore breasts, rubbing and soothing the aching buds.

A moment later, lightning blazed across her poor abused clit. Then Johnny's fingers were there, rubbing and soothing her clit. It was almost enough to send her over the edge again. "Oh God." She whined, back arching. "I can't."

"You can." Johnny growled and thrust his hips up into her.

"Fuuuuck. She keened as she tumbled over the edge again. She collapsed forward against Johnny's chest, body shuddering. That's when the real fucking began. Before she could catch her breath, Derrick's hands gripped her face as he lined up his cock. It was in her mouth and pushing into her throat a moment later.

Kevin's hands squeezed her hips, and Johnny's grabbed her upper thighs. Together they railed her. She was nothing but a vessel for the three of them to use. And use her they did. It did not take them long to bring her poor tortured body to yet another orgasm. She could barely moan as her body trembled.

Her jaw ached. Her eyelids drooped. She went completely boneless.

Kevin pulled out of her ass first, his warm cum coating her a moment later.

She barely registered it.

When Johnny suddenly pushed her upright and sat up, Derrick's cock popped from her mouth. She felt the bed dip as Johnny got on his knees before her, warm spurts of cum splattering her belly. "Fuck yeah." Johnny groaned, painting her with his cum.

"Bring her closer," Derrick rasped. Hands gripped her upper arms and maneuvered her body so she was leaning forward again. "Open your mouth, baby girl," Derrick ordered before warm globs of cum splashed across her face and tits, getting in her mouth and running down her neck.

She swallowed what she could, but she was covered completely in cum. She was a hot, sticky mess, and she was too exhausted to complain. She was lowered gently onto her side, and the ropes tugged on her arms before she was quickly untied.

They sat her up slowly and inspected her arms. They rubbed at her muscles and rotated her shoulders while slowly stretching her, massaging what they could around the cast. Blood flow slowly returned to the limbs, and Kara sighed, still feeling boneless.

She was a filthy mess and could really use a shower. The blindfold was still in place though, so the scene had not ended. Thankfully it kept her from seeing the rivers of cum her men had shot all over her. She let the guys fuss over and take care of her, vaguely wondering when or if they would clean her off.

A camera snapped another picture. She was sure she looked like a used, dirty whore. She would smile at the thought if she weren't so damn tired. Instead, she let them move her and position her. Hands rubbed through the cum coating her skin, rubbing it in like lotion. "So there's no mistaking just who you belong to." Johnny growled.

Chapter Twenty-One

T HE NEXT MORNING KARA smiled as she slowly came awake. She knew she was alone, vaguely remembering the kisses pressed to her forehead and lips as her boys left early to go to work. She had rolled over and gone back to sleep, her body still exhausted from their strenuous and animalistic sexathon.

She'd felt thoroughly used and debauched by the time they had shot cum all over her and had rubbed it into her skin. Marking her. Claiming her.

She'd gone to bed dirty and woken up feeling great.

It was late morning when she finally dragged herself out of bed and took a shower. Feeling sentimental, she showered with Johnny's bodywash, not quite wanting to let go of the ownership they'd claimed the night before.

It had been the hottest and most feral erotic experience of her life.

Afterward, she had felt closer to her boys than ever before. Smelling like Johnny was one more little piece that she could hold on to. She would have to talk to them about moving her big bed over to Johnny's and all sleeping together from now on.

After her shower, she ate a quick brunch before she answered the door for her assistant Stacy and Marlie, Bandit's old lady. Kara had finally asked for help going through all the boxes, and who better to help her than those who already technically worked for her?

Kara was deep in thought when the phone call came in. Stacy nudged her and handed her the cell phone. Kara grinned when she saw it was Kevin on the phone and quickly answered it. "Hey sexy." She smirked, looking down at her papers.

"Babe, we've got problems," Kevin said immediately, getting straight to the point.

Her head shot up and she looked at Marlie. "What kind of problems?"

"I'll tell you about it when you get here, but Derrick was shot—"

"What do you mean Derrick was shot?!" Kara jumped out of her chair, wincing slightly at the twinge of pain in her ribs, and headed for the door. Being tied up the night before had been fun but had slightly aggravated her healing ribs.

"I'll drive," Marlie said, grabbing her things quickly.

Kara didn't pay her much mind and slipped her feet into flip-flops, grabbing her keys off the hook. She turned the lock on the door handle and headed outside. Marlie and Stacy followed.

"He's OK. He will be OK, but he's lost a lot of blood. He's asking for you." Kevin sighed, sounding tense.

Kara tried to read between the lines, but her mind was only conjuring up horrible thoughts. She quickly climbed into Marlie's Jeep Wrangler. "What do you mean he lost a lot of blood? Are you taking him to the hospital?"

"Can't do that, babe." Kevin sighed.

"What the fuck do you mean you can't do that?" she demanded, her mind racing.

"Kara, just get to the clubhouse. I'll see you soon. I love you," Kevin said.

"I love you too." Kara sighed and ended the call. She turned to Marlie, who was throwing the Jeep into reverse.

"How bad?" Marlie asked as she backed down the driveway.

"He didn't say. He said Derrick was shot, that he was OK and that he would be OK, and that he lost a lot of blood." Kara sighed, running her fingers through her hair.

Marlie nodded as she pulled out onto the street and threw the transmission into drive, peeling out and heading down the street. "I knew shit was kicking up with the Psychos, but fuck," Marlie muttered.

"They told me it was nothing they couldn't handle," Kara muttered.

Marlie made a grunt of annoyance.

"Your boyfriend was shot?" Stacy asked from the back seat.

Kara jumped and shouted. She turned in her seat to find her assistant holding on for dear life in the back seat, while Marlie raced them toward the clubhouse. "Stacy, shit! You damn near gave me a heart attack!" Kara shouted, holding her hand over her racing heart.

Stacy didn't look startled, though—she looked nervous and unsure. "What happened?" she asked, pressing the issue.

Kara shook her head. "I don't know. Kevin just said to get to the clubhouse. Fuck, Stacy." Kara groaned. "You don't know what you're walking into. You should have gone home."

Stacy shook her head firmly. "I'm staying."

Kara eyed her assistant warily. It wasn't that she didn't trust Stacy, because she did—with her life. Stacy was literally helping her go after her father. Over the years, she'd always been on Kara's side whenever there was an issue with her father over the years.

But this was different. This was the world of the Ravager Knights, and Kara was still figuring out if she herself belonged in it. It was dark and gritty. People got hurt or killed. Things happened that didn't happen to normal people.

Kara nodded once.

It wasn't long before they were flying through the open gates of the compound. Marlie didn't even come to a complete stop before Kara was launching herself out of the Jeep and into Kevin's arms. "Easy," he muttered, holding her tight.

She pulled away quickly. "Where is he?" she asked, looking up at Kevin, seeing the exhaustion weighing on him.

"Come on." He sighed and grabbed her hand.

She followed him into the clubhouse, passing brothers and their wives. She met worried gazes while in a daze. She didn't fully comprehend the situation yet.

Kevin pulled her through the main room of the clubhouse to the hallway beyond. They headed up the stairs and down the hall toward Johnny's room but stopped two doors short of it at an open door.

Inside, a doctor was telling Johnny how to care for the wound, but all Kara could see was Derrick. He was propped up in a queen-size bed that looked too small for his large body. He was shirtless and covered in blood.

She barely saw the white bandage before she gasped and moved into the room.

Johnny whipped around when he heard her gasp. "Princess." He sighed, moving toward her and trying to block her way to Derrick.

She stopped moving when she saw that Johnny was covered in blood too. She tentatively reached out for him, her hand shaking.

"I'm OK," he murmured and pulled her closer. She gripped his leather cut as he leaned down to kiss her. "He's OK," Johnny murmured against her lips.

She pulled away from him and looked around him to see Derrick. He was watching her with half-lidded eyes. Kara ignored the doctor as she walked by him. She slowed to a stop at Derrick's bedside, taking him in. His chest rose and fell slowly, his dark brown hair was a wreck, and his thick brown beard was matted with blood. There was a white bandage on his right bicep that contrasted with his tanned skin.

Tears welled in her eyes as she stared down at him. "Hey, baby girl." Derrick's voice was raspy.

A sob broke out, and she quickly raised her hand to stifle it.

"Come 'ere," Derrick rasped. He lifted his left arm toward her.

She went quickly, rounding the bed to the far side. She kicked off her flip-flops and carefully crawled across the bed toward him. She was careful not to jostle him as she slid against his side. He wrapped his arm around her and pulled her tight against him.

"Shhh," he murmured and kissed the crown of her head.

Her sobs shook her body. She felt the bed dip behind her and a moment later, Kevin was curled around her back. Derrick pressed a kiss to her forehead before he drifted off, passing out from the painkillers.

When she finally calmed down, she rolled over carefully and faced Kevin. He was propped up on his elbow and brushed her hair back from her face. She was sure she looked a hot mess. Her eyes were probably swollen, her face red, but none of that ever mattered to Kevin. He looked down at her with all the love in the world in his eyes.

"What happened?" she asked him.

"Devil's Psychos, down by the docks," Johnny answered from across the room.

She lifted her head to see him leaning against the doorframe. He had showered and dressed in a white T-shirt and raggedy jeans. His feet were bare. The sight would have made her smile had the situation not been so serious.

"You told me the tension was nothing to worry about, that 'it was nothing you couldn't handle.'" She quoted him, speaking of their conversation the night before.

Kevin sighed next to her, and Johnny nodded slowly. He pushed off the doorframe and walked toward the bed. He took a seat at the foot of the bed and grabbed her foot, holding on to her. "I know, I did say that. Things changed." Johnny sighed, running a hand over his skull trimmed hair. "They're getting more ambitious."

Kara frowned, not fully understanding what was going on. "Because of the trade routes?" she asked.

Johnny shrugged.

"We don't really know." Kevin sighed, running his hand down her back. "Could be trade routes."

"Could be that they're greedy motherfuckers trying to push in on our territory," Johnny snapped back.

Kara didn't say anything; there was nothing for her to add. This was a far different world than she was used to. "So what exactly happened with Derrick?"

"It was a shoot-out; they ambushed us during a pickup. Somehow they knew about our shipment," Johnny elaborated while his hand rubbed circles into the arch of her foot.

Kara narrowed her eyes and looked up at Johnny. "A mole?"

Johnny shrugged. "Not sure. Possibly. There was a spy the other night at the compound. It's possible he overheard something. It's possible they've been spying for a lot longer than we knew." Johnny let out a frustrated sigh and laid back on the bed.

The queen-size mattress was a tight fit for the four of them, especially with Derrick sprawled out, injured and knocked the fuck out. Kara spread her legs and made room for Johnny to squeeze his top half between her legs. He rested his head on her belly.

She stroked her hand over his skull trimmed hair as she slid her leg over his torso. Once she was relatively comfortable, she sighed and looked over her shoulder at Derrick.

"Don't worry, babe," Kevin murmured. "He'll be OK. It was a through and through and didn't hit bone. It's his nondominant hand. He'll be able to rest the shoulder and arm long enough to heal it quickly."

"Force him into a sling and you'll get to baby him." Johnny smirked against the bare skin of her belly, as her shirt had ridden up.

Kara smiled at the thought. "I'll take care of him," she mumbled.

"Take a nap, babe," Kevin mumbled and pressed a kiss to her forehead. "We'll be here when you wake up."

Kara smiled sleepily and nodded. "Maybe just a short one," she conceded.

When Kara woke, Johnny and Kevin were gone. She rolled over to find Derrick still passed out, but someone had cleaned the dried blood from his chest and beard while she had been sleeping.

She snuggled closer to him, resting her head on his shoulder while trying not to jostle the bed too much. She had no idea how much pain he would be in when he woke up. She assumed the doc had given him some good painkillers.

She wasn't upset that Johnny and Kevin were gone. She was almost grateful for the time alone with Derrick. She couldn't wait to get him home and into their bed. It may not have been the Alaskan king from her house, but it was still a king and bigger than the queen in his dorm room.

She would have to talk to Johnny and her boys about the future and their plans. She'd been dealing with insurance from the house fire, but it would still be a long time before Johnny's crew could get in there and start working.

Would she even still want to move back into her place after spending so much time with her guys? Would they care if she moved in permanently? The last conversation she had with Johnny made it seem like she was staying. She would have to talk to all of them about it before she went and ordered a new mattress for Johnny's room and had the guys bring the frame of the old bed over from her house.

Derrick groaned beneath her.

She eased off him and looked up to see him blinking back at her. "Hey," she said softly.

He smiled faintly. "Hey, baby girl." His voice was raspy.

"How's the pain? Can I get you anything?" she asked, feeling unsure. She wasn't used to taking care of anyone, just as she'd never had anyone take care of her before Johnny and Kevin and Derrick.

Derrick shifted and pulled his good arm from between them; she had been resting her head on his shoulder. He wrapped it around her back and pulled her into him. She went easily, resting her head on his chest as he held her close. "I'm good, baby girl. I'm sorry I scared you."

She sighed heavily and let her body relax further against his side, draping her arm over his chest. "You really did scare me," she admitted.

His hand tightened on her waist, but he didn't say anything.

She carried on, needing to get her feelings off her chest. Her heart ached and her nerves were still shot to shit. "When Kevin called, I'd never been so scared in my life," she said, shifting so she could look up at him. "The thought of something happening to you—that I might lose you—" She broke off on a sob and buried her face into his chest.

"Baby girl." Derrick sighed, holding her tighter. "I'm fine. A little bullet isn't going to keep me down." He tried to joke.

It only made her sob harder into his chest. "I just kept thinking the worst." She gasped. "And all I could think was what-if?" She lifted her head off his chest and propped herself on her elbow so she could look down at him. "What if you died and you didn't know how much I love you? Because Derrick, I fucking love you, and I don't know that I could live without you," she admitted, tears falling down her face.

Derrick's green eyes blazed as he wrapped his fingers around the back of her neck and yanked her face down to his. She went willingly as he devoured her mouth with his. She groaned as he poured his love into the kiss. Her eyes closed as she shifted over him, throwing her leg over his hips and straddling him.

She let her weight drop onto his lower body, and he groaned into her mouth. "Fuck, baby girl." He moaned.

"I don't want to hurt you," she murmured against his lips.

"You're gonna hurt my balls if you don't do something about that teasin'." He chuckled.

She grinned and ground her core down on his rock-hard erection. "This teasin'?" She smirked.

"Little slut, you're walking a fine line." Derrick's voice rumbled.

She smirked again and pressed an open-mouthed kiss to the center of his left pectoral and bit down a little.

He groaned, eliciting a chuckle from her.

"I don't think you're in any position to boss me around, my love." She giggled and kissed her way down his washboard abs.

"Little slut, if you think I can't bend you over my lap and spank that ass, you better think again." Derrick growled, his fingers fisting her hair.

She giggled and sucked a hickey into his abs, just above his jeans, chuckling when he groaned and arched into her. She made quick work of undoing his jeans and wasn't surprised to find he was commando beneath them. She pulled them down his legs and tossed them to the floor.

She kissed her way back up his legs, nibbling his inner thigh before she did the same to the other leg.

"Baby girl." He groaned. "You're killing me."

She chuckled as she palmed the base of his cock and wrapped her lips around the head.

"Ah, fuck." He groaned, throwing his head back against the pillows.

She swallowed him down, sliding her hand from his base and cupping his balls. She sucked deep and he groaned again. Her tongue swirled his head before she flicked her tongue expertly against his frenulum. Over and over.

"Holy mother of God." He groaned and arched upward. He let out a low hiss and his fingers tightened in her hair. "Again," he ordered.

She didn't hesitate. Her tongue flicked and licked against his most sensitive parts, and she reveled in his moans.

"So fucking talented, baby girl," he rasped.

She swallowed him down as far as she could, wishing her right hand and wrist weren't still wrapped in a cast. Her left caressed and massaged his balls while she sucked and swirled over his head.

His groans grew louder.

Pride swelled within her knowing she could unravel her man so quickly.

Before he could come, he roughly pulled her up by her hair. "Kara, stop."

She wiped her mouth as she pulled off him. "What's wrong?" she asked, seeing the distress on his face.

He was panting uncontrollably, his head pressed back against the pillows. "Nothing. I just want to come in that tight pussy."

She smirked and leaned down, flicking his head with her tongue once more.

His hand wrapped around her jaw roughly. "Be a good girl," he ordered, holding her in place.

She kept her gaze locked on his bright green eyes.

"Climb on my cock," he ordered and let go of her jaw.

She moved quickly, sliding from the bed. She shimmied out of her blue jean shorts and lace undies before she was back on the bed straddling him. She didn't bother to take off her tank top or bra.

Derrick's hands grabbed her hips the minute she was close enough. He guided her over him. Wasting little time, she reached between their bodies and grabbed his cock. She slid his head along her slit, slicking him with her arousal before she lined him up and slowly sank down on his thick length.

"That's it." He groaned, his eyes fluttering closed.

Kara swiveled her hips slowly and watched his handsome face as pleasure rolled over him. His thick mane of auburn hair was a halo around his head on the pillows, and his beard was as bushy as ever. He was glorious in a rough-and-tumble, lumberjack kind of way, and she absolutely loved that about him.

She loved everything about him: all his goofy anecdotes and silly jokes. He was always making her laugh and was quick to put a smile on her face. He was sweet and caring and 100% hers.

She rested her left hand on his pec and set the pace, riding him. Usually, she would rest both hands on his chest, but with his injury and her cast, she didn't want to hurt him. "You're holding back." He growled and then tried to slam her down on his cock only to groan and let go of her with his right hand—his injured side.

"Fuck." She sighed, leaning over him.

Pain rippled across his face.

"I'm sorry," she cried, stopping. She braced her left hand on the bed above his shoulders and waited.

"I'm OK." He breathed.

"Maybe we should wait." She hedged, knowing it was the last thing either of them wanted at that moment.

"Hell no." He growled and snapped his hips up—his abs apparently worked perfectly.

She slid her hips up and down and gasped as the new position pressed her clit against his pubic bone. She did it again and again, finding a rhythm and fucking him with all she had.

"That's it, baby girl." He groaned. His good hand was still on her hip, resting there. He dug his fingers into her skin roughly.

She took her time and set her pace. Sweat slid between her still-clothed breasts and down her back. She didn't care. She swiveled her hips, and Derrick swore. She smirked and did it again. "So fucking gorgeous, Kara," Derrick muttered.

She threw her head back and groaned as her orgasm crashed over her. She rolled her hips and moaned when Derrick's thrust up to meet hers, riding her through her high.

He held her steady with his good arm, while he thrust into her, grunting and following her over the edge. "Fuck." He growled, his body shuddering beneath her.

She rested her forehead against his chest, careful not to aggravate his gunshot wound, while she caught her breath. "I'm not hurting you, am I?" she asked softly.

His hands circled her waist, one sliding up her back under her shirt. "No baby. You could never hurt me," he murmured. His voice was soft, as if he was fading into sleep again. "I love you."

Her smile was wide, and she knew everything would be OK. "I love you too."

Chapter Twenty-two

THE NEXT DAY, KARA pored over documents in the dining room. The house was full of her team members: Marlie and Stacy along with Danvers and his assistant, Gina. They were digging through the boxes with renewed vigor. She needed to find anything she could on Case Holdings and anything that linked her father to the crimes he was framing Mac for.

Derrick was propped up on the couch in the great room. He was watching a movie and scrolling through his phone when he wasn't napping. He'd refused to stay in bed despite her arguing with him. She had given up when he said he'd wanted to be close to her while she was working. She would be able to keep an eye on him at least. Kara found herself grateful for his stubbornness throughout the morning. Whenever she found her anxiety kicking in over the thought of almost losing him, she was able to look over and see him in the flesh instead of worrying how he was doing upstairs.

Danvers was on his best behavior, too, while Derrick was present. Not that Kara ever really worried about Danvers, but he tended to be overtly condescending at times when it was just Kara and him. He was a bit of a celebrity defense attorney in Mourningside, and though Kara was a kickass corporate attorney in her own right, only criminal defense lawyers seemed to matter to Danvers.

She had rolled her eyes and told him she'd studied the same law books he had. He eventually got over himself when they were speaking, but with Derrick on the couch, Danvers hadn't even bothered with his usual posturing. It was a relief.

Marlie and Stacy were godsends when it came to research. They already knew her system, knew the company's filing system, and were able to quickly teach Gina and Danvers.

They had made quick work of a year's worth of boxes. It wasn't until they reached the end of the first year that they found anything of value. "Got something," Marlie said.

Kara looked up from her files to see a smile on Marlie's face. "What's that?"

"Case Holdings state filing papers, for the incorporation," Marlie elaborated, flipping through the file in her hands. "Incorporation papers, the business license, the SS-4 form from the IRS. All of it."

Kara's heart leaped into her throat. She rounded the table at the same time as Danvers, and together, they pored over the documents. Sure enough, her father's name was all over the papers right next to Mac's.

"Holy shit." She gasped, reading the filing dates. "This is it!" She looked up at Danvers, who didn't share her same enthusiasm.

"It's a good start." He nodded. "Which box did you find those in?"

Things moved quickly from there, the four of them abandoning the files they had in their hands to help pore over the other files in Marlie's box. They found a gold mine of information: the banking forms signed by both parties, the original business plan with handwritten notes from both of them, and the W-9. She immediately recognized her father's neat handwriting. She assumed the other handwriting was Mac's.

"This is everything I need," Danvers murmured, looking through the file.

"You can build a case around this?" Kara questioned, knowing she herself probably could.

"Absolutely. Let's keep digging; there's bound to be more," he muttered, staring down at the papers.

They quickly got back to work, diving into the next box.

Hours later, they assembled a full box of documents that clearly detailed Vince Carmichael and Mac Taylor's going into business together. They found documents dated a year later with only

Vince's signature. There was a clear paper trail that showed Case Holdings being placed in a trust.

An hour later, they had it.

They had everything they needed and then some.

They found all the registration papers for Case Holdings with her father's and Mac's signatures. They had the documents on Candy Creek Inc., a company that was solely in her father's name, proving her father was paying himself via Case Holdings and charging Carmichael and Associates' clients for research.

From there, the money was moved to Candle-Carla Trust and then on to Carlita Associates, where Vince Carmichael and Ken Laraway were listed as owners of the law firm in the Caymans. Her father was using her mother's name to run all of his dirty dealings.

Stephanie had found thousands of instances where her father and several other senior partners had billed Case Holdings for research. Carmichael and Associates had paid out millions.

The actual sum was astronomical.

"This is everything we've needed," Kara said, finally sitting down for a minute to take a break and let the reality wash over her.

"This is fucking illegal." Marlie grumbled as she pored over documents, still finding more incriminating evidence.

"We have our case." Danvers nodded at Kara.

Kara gave him a rare smile; he'd been oddly fun to work with. Despite his cocky attitude, he was a great research partner and dug in deep. Gina was just as great. Too good for him, for sure.

Marlie and Stacy made Kara feel like she'd never left the office. "You're both getting raises when I get back," Kara told them.

"Who says I wanna work for you again?" Stacy shot back immediately.

Kara grinned. "You won't have a choice."

Stacy rolled her eyes and continued working.

They had everything they needed, but they wanted to finish out the year of boxes they had, to be thorough. They would need to continue to go through all the other boxes in her off-site warehouse, but they had some breathing room now.

They had enough to bring her father in front of a judge and indict him. They could get the warrant issued and have him held without bond as a flight risk due to the offshore bank accounts.

She just needed to make sure Carmichael and Associates would still be standing afterward. Thankfully, when her father had retired last year and named her managing partner, he had to put her name on the deed and legally sign everything over to her.

That could make things tricky when it came time to testify, but as most of the dirty dealings happened before she was even born, she would likely be in the clear. She also had Stephanie's report to show that Case Holdings had never been listed as a research firm on any of the cases that Kara had worked on.

Stephanie had painted a pretty clear picture of who at the firm was involved and who wasn't. Unfortunately, it was most of the senior partners—the old-school crowd that had worshiped her father. She had slowly been firing them in the last year, working her way through her father's old stalwarts—but it was too little, too late.

When it was time to call it a day, the girls headed out, leaving Kara alone with Danvers, or as alone as they could get with Derrick propped up on the couch, watching TV and keeping an eye on them.

Danvers was still reading a file, glasses propped on his nose.

"Whatcha got there?" Kara asked softly, not wanting Derrick to hear from across the great room. He had been dozing off and on all day against his stack of pillows.

Freddy looked up from the file with a frown on his face. His gray eyes were missing their usual cocky glint. "I found the motive," he murmured, keeping his voice low. He sat up straight before he held the file out to Kara.

She reached for it, but Danvers held on to his side, looking her dead in the eye. "You can make a copy, but I'll need this," he said, his voice stern.

She nodded, and he slowly surrendered the file.

He stood up and started gathering everything he was taking with him. Every day he took more and more back to his office for safekeeping.

Kara opened the file and started reading. She got lost in the documents while Danvers pulled on his Tom Ford suit jacket and buttoned it.

She let out a quiet gasp as she realized what she was reading. Paternity Test Results.

Mac Taylor was her brother Marcos's father. Marcos Candela's parents were Carlita Candela and Mac Taylor.

She and Marcos had different dads.

Vince never lied to her regarding the paternity test results. Carlita had lied to both Mac and Vince. Had she been hoping that Vince would take care of her and the baby? Had she hoped to pull a fast one on him? Use him for his money?

Kara didn't know. She didn't know a lot anymore. Apparently, her mother was not the woman Kara had thought she was. Carlita held a secret past that she'd kept from her daughter, kept from both her children.

"Shit." Kara breathed, reading the file. She looked up at Danvers in shock as the reality of it all came crashing down on her, as everything she'd ever known as a child came down and settled on her shoulders. The weight of it made breathing harder.

Danvers nodded. "Make yourself a copy, but then I need the original." He continued gathering his things.

Kara nodded. "This is huge."

"You have no idea," Danvers answered, shaking his head. "I suggest you talk to your brother about that, and don't wait." Danvers leveled her with piercing stare that sent a shiver running down her spine.

He knows something.

She narrowed her eyes at him. She didn't like mind games. If he knew something, he better just spill. "Spit it out, Danvers."

"Talk to your brother." He gave her a pointed stare before he turned and headed for the door.

Kara glared after him, but short of chasing him and causing a scene in front of Derrick—something she really didn't want to do—she was at a loss. She turned back to the file instead, still in disbelief.

Marcos and Johnny are half brothers.

Chapter Twenty-Three

OVER THE COURSE OF the next week, Kara found herself constantly forcing her thoughts away from Marcos and what they'd discovered. She zoned out while reading through case notes, her thoughts a foggy cloud that weighed on her mind. Danvers, for all his cocky bullshit, didn't comment other than to reiterate that she needed to speak with her brother.

Her brother Marcos. How would she tell her brother about his father? How would she tell her brother that he had a brother? That she was dating his brother?

Noticing her preoccupation, her men had assumed she was feeling overwhelmed by the uptick in fighting with the Devil's Psychos—thought that she was scared and worried about the fallout after Derrick's getting shot.

She didn't have the heart to tell them otherwise. She couldn't stand the thought of telling Johnny about his father being Marcos's father—telling him that Marcos was his brother.

Anytime she thought she might be able to say something, to bring it up in some roundabout way, a phone would ring and more bad news would come their way—another skirmish would kick up between the Ravager Knights and the Devil's Psychos, another issue in the trade routes and war—and any chance she might have had to come clean about what she had learned went out the window.

Her boys had been right, though, when they assumed she'd been rattled after Derrick was shot. She was rattled. When she wasn't staring off into space, she was waiting on Derrick hand and foot.

She'd set him up on the couch in the great room when she was working with Danvers and her team, easily accessible should he need anything. And other than snacks here or there or something to drink, Derrick had been content to just watch TV, play on his phone, or watch her.

He'd driven her crazy with his staring across the room at all hours of the day. He'd told her she was working too hard again and asked if she needed another reminder of how to take it easy.

She had brushed him off, told him they needed to file with the DA soon.

Despite Derrick backing off and no longer questioning her, she had a feeling he didn't buy her explanation. He had been there when Danvers left her that file. He had seen the change in her since that pivotal moment in time. He had to have heard parts of their conversation, if not read the body language.

It was a moment that would forever be seared into her brain as the day everything changed, as the day her family changed.

Johnny and Kevin had immersed themselves in the club while Derrick recovered. They left the construction company in the hands of their foremen while they stepped away to handle the retaliation against the Psychos.

Saturday morning, Derrick got out of bed and rolled his injured shoulder. When he rotated his arm and shoulder a full 360 degrees, he stood up and grinned. "I'm going for a ride. Who's coming with me?" he declared. He was half out of the bedroom before Kara even realized what he had said.

"The hell you are!" Kara shouted after him, scrambling to untangle herself from the sheets in their massive bed.

Johnny chuckled from the master bathroom where he'd been brushing his teeth.

Kara didn't hear Kevin as she ran after Derrick in nothing but one of the guys'—Kevin's—T-shirts she'd slipped over her head in the middle of the night.

Derrick was laughing as he headed back to his bedroom buck naked, his pale ass gleaming in the sunlight shining through the wall of windows on the open balcony hallway. "Get dressed, baby girl. We're going out." He smirked over his shoulder at her.

"Derrick," she snapped, anger and fear simmering in her belly. "You can't be serious! It's only been a week. You can't ride a motorcycle yet!"

Derrick entered his bedroom and flipped on the light switch. "Who said anything about the bike?" He smirked at her as he opened a dresser drawer.

She paused, her mouth opening. "What?" she asked.

He smirked again and pulled out a plain black T-shirt. "Speechless, huh? Usually, we have to give you at *least* three orgasms before we can get you nonverbal." There was that cocky as fuck smirk again.

Her heart raced; she loved that smirk and cocky attitude so much—she'd told him as much. Told him she loved him whenever she could, as she did all her boys now that the cat was out of the bag, now that she knew they loved her too.

"My love." Derrick took a deep breath once he was fully dressed. He pulled her into his arms and sat on the bed with her straddling his lap. "I love you, I do, but if I stay in this house a moment longer, I am going to kill someone."

She laughed and laughed and finally agreed. She would do anything for this man, anything for her three insane and cocky boys who loved to drive her crazy. And they would do anything for her—had already done so much for her in the last three months they'd been together.

She could only hope they would still love her after she told them the truth.

Johnny couldn't keep the smile off his face as sat at the picnic table with his boys and the love of his life. The August sun shone down brightly on them as they ate their lunch at a picnic table at Quinnlyn Beach.

Kara had on a pink terry cloth summer dress that hugged her curves like a second skin. He'd smacked her ass when he saw it in that soft dress. Plump perfection, just waiting to be bent over the tailgate of his truck. Or the picnic table.

He wasn't picky. He just needed to watch his cock disappear between those glorious plump globes of that fine, fine ass.

Johnny had been almost glad when Derrick had deemed his shoulder not quite strong enough to ride yet—Kara could wear a dress or a skirt and not feel the need for jeans to ride.

Kevin had only smirked at him and called shotgun in Johnny's truck.

Kara, when she'd heard they weren't riding, had opted for the pretty pink number she was rocking that made her golden tanned skin appear even darker. Her blond hair was down around her shoulders, and a pair of sunglasses were perched on her cute button nose.

She had come alive once Johnny had pulled into the beach parking lot. The late summer heat was still hanging on during the day, the evening temps had cooled off the lake past the point of them daring to swim. It hadn't mattered to Kara, though, as she had quickly walked into the cool water until it was up to her knees. Her skirt came to midthigh, leaving several inches of bare skin below the hemline.

Johnny loved watching her smile and laugh while she splashed in the water with Derrick and Kevin, loved seeing her let loose after a stressful week of working nonstop.

He wasn't stupid; he knew something had changed this week. Derrick had told him she'd found something, that Danvers had given her something, and ever since that moment she had been distant with them. She'd withdrawn slightly, as if the weight of the world rested on her slim shoulders.

He thought about bringing it up, asking her directly, but decided it could wait. He didn't want to ruin this moment. This beautiful, peaceful lunch with his best friends and the love of his life. He wished he could bottle up this serenity and bask in its glory whenever life got too hard.

Kara shot him a bright smile from across the table. She had caught him staring at her. Again. As she had caught them all staring at her whenever she wasn't paying attention. As if they couldn't believe she was theirs. Like if they blinked, she'd be gone.

Kara felt lighter than she had in a long while—all week, in fact.

Quinnlyn Beach was beautiful with the crystal-clear water of Lake White Buffalo and the soft white sand that came from the natural limestone walls that made up one side of the beach. In the summer, teens and college kids drove up to those cliffs—Dead Man's Bluff—to make out and party, and those who were daring enough even jumped from those cliffs into the water below.

The limestone walls jutted out into the lake, making a sharp ninety-degree angle for boaters to navigate when on the water. It created a clashing of the currents, with lots of water-skiers and tubers hitting the rough waters and wiping out from hitting the waves wrong, hence the name Dead Man's Pointe.

Too many accidents had led to regulations for boaters towing skiers and tubers, so Dead's Man's Pointe wouldn't be so deadly. It didn't stop the kids from having fun, though.

"This was a good idea." Kara smiled as they slowly packed up their remaining food and garbage.

"Glad you let me out of the house after all?" Derrick smirked at her.

She rolled her eyes. "Maybe I'll tie you to the bed next time instead," she shot back him.

His smirk turned lethal as his hand came out and grabbed her ass. "Baby girl, you wanna tie me up, all you gotta do is ask." He swatted her ass with a loud smack.

She jumped slightly, looking around. There were families nearby. Children. She didn't want to make a spectacle. Thankfully no one was paying attention. "I'm gonna hit the bathroom before we head out," she declared, gathering up their garbage to take with her.

"Sounds good, baby girl." Derrick nodded.

She dumped their trash into a garbage can outside the bathhouse before she headed inside to do her business. While she was sitting on the toilet, she answered some text messages from Marlie and Danvers and even one from Rachel asking if she was going to come by the club with the guys for whatever party they had planned that evening.

She took her time, enjoying the cool air in the bathroom. She knew she should hurry, that her boys would worry, but she liked making people wait. So she texted Rachel that she wasn't sure yet and would let her know after she talked to the guys.

When she finally left the bathroom after washing her hands, her boys were no longer at the picnic table. She looked around, and her heart dropped into her belly when she saw the three of them toe to toe with a large group of Devil's Psychos in the parking lot.

Three against ten. Johnny was squared off in front, with Kevin and Derrick slightly behind and flanking him. Kara didn't know what to do. They hadn't talked about this before. Should she stay away? Would it be better for her to stay in the bathroom? What if someone came for her? Would it be better if she was with her guys?

Fuck. She couldn't hear what was being said from where she stood. She took a deep breath and squared her shoulders. She would go over there and hope for the best. As she headed toward the group of leather-clad bikers, their voices grew louder.

"That why you killed our brother?" Johnny growled, getting into the face of one of the Devil's Psychos.

Kara locked eyes with Kevin, and he quickly pulled her behind him.

"What do we have here? Aren't you just a pretty little piece of bubble gum." A Psycho sneered as he raked his eyes down Kara's body.

She rolled her eyes and glared at him. Men like him were disgusting.

"You're in our territory," one of the Psychos ground out.

"Quinnlyn Beach is neutral ground. Families come here," Kevin shot back.

The Psycho, a man with short brown hair and black eyes, smirked back. "Well, you have to go through our territory to get here, so we've claimed it as ours," he drawled.

Derrick growled. "The hell you have. This is Knights territory, and Quinnlyn Beach is off-limits."

One of the guys laughed. It was sinister and sent shivers down Kara's spine. She didn't like the way they were leering at her. She looked over the group of rough-and-tumble men. Most of them were around her age, maybe older. Mid-to-late thirties. Not all of them leered at her, though. Most of them were too busy watching her boys. They were smart: she knew with all her being that Kevin, Johnny, and Derrick would fight like hell to defend her. They would do everything in their power to keep her safe. Still, if she didn't need to be in a situation like this, she wouldn't go out of her way to find one.

She would feel a whole hell of a lot better if the odds were a little more balanced. Or if the douchebags in front of them would back the fuck off.

She didn't hear the roar of the motorcycles until it was too late. She didn't see the additional Devil's Psychos coming until the crowd before her parted like the Red Sea. The wall of leather stepped back to reveal her goddamn brother: Marcos.

"You got a lot of fucking nerve, Candela." Johnny growled, getting in her brother's face.

Kara had never seen her brother so angry. "Fuck you, Taylor," Marcos spat.

Kara took in her brother. The black, close-shaven hair that glinted in the fading sunlight. The black T-shirt and blue jeans that she saw him wear every day when they were growing up. The heavy black boots that were another staple of her brother's wardrobe. The familiar mirrored sunglasses and the black bandanna that was tied in a one-inch band around his forehead. The heavy piercings in his ears.

What she was not familiar with was the heavy black leather cut he wore over his T-shirt. The cut that had a Devil's Psychos patch on the right side of his chest and, below that, another that read vice president.

"What the fuck?" Kara breathed, stepping out from behind Kevin. She stepped around him so that when Marcos looked over Johnny's large shoulder, he saw her. "Marcos?"

She couldn't see his eyes behind his mirrored sunglasses. Couldn't see if it was anger or disbelief that colored his eyes as he froze and shut his mouth. He went utterly still as he watched her walk around Kevin and Johnny.

She pushed Johnny's hand out of the way when he tried to push her back behind him. He clearly didn't want her anywhere near the Devil's Psychos. But he didn't know, did he? Because Kara herself hadn't known. Her brother was a goddamn Devil's Psycho. Her brother was in an MC.

"Kara?" Marcos asked.

"What the fuck is this?" she exclaimed, stepping in front of Johnny.

Johnny's hands landed on her hips, his fingers digging in.

Marcos took off his sunglasses and eyed her warily. She watched him as his eyes roamed over every inch of her in her skintight dress, Johnny's hands on her hips. Johnny pressed against her back, and Derrick and Kevin flanked them.

She watched as Marcos put together the pieces before him—as he remembered their last conversation after she got out of the hospital and the conversation before that one, when they had fought before her attack—and the dawning realization of just *who* had been railing his sister crashed down on him.

She didn't give him a chance to speak before she laid into him. "Since when the fuck are you in a motorcycle club, big brother?"

She watched as the ripple went around the group as her words struck home. Watched the dawning horror and then anger slide over the group of Devil's Psychos. Felt Johnny stiffen behind her as he, too, learned the truth for the first time.

Marcos swallowed but he didn't say a word, just stared at her in shocked horror. She wondered if he had ever planned on telling her the truth or if he'd planned to keep her in the dark all this time.

She looked over his shoulder as the crowd behind him stirred and two more ghosts from her past were revealed in the crowd. Her brother's two best friends stood behind him: Jason Langford and Nico Gage. Both men also had on black leather cuts bearing Devil's Psychos patches.

"Hey, Jason. Nico." She nodded at the two men.

"Hey, Kare Bear." Jason smiled ruefully at her, his blond hair shining in the sunlight. The barbell through his eyebrow glinted above his steel-colored eyes. He had always been kind to her growing up. He was never mean to her even when she was an annoying little sister, tagging along with them everywhere.

"Hey, *Manita*." Nico smiled sadly. Despite his Italian heritage, he was as blond and blue-eyed as Johnny. His skin, though, was a deep golden brown that showed both his heritage and his long hours in the sun.

Kara's gaze turned back to her brother and she waited. She leaned back against Johnny and rested her hands over his, lacing their fingers together over her lower belly. His large hands spanned the width of her hips.

Marcos's dark eyes rested on her face. She could see the regret and pain in his eyes over the last words they had spoken to each other. She hadn't seen him since before her accident. He may have visited her while she was unconscious, but he hadn't tried to see her once she'd been released. "Let's go." Marcos motioned to his guys. "Roll out."

Kara didn't move as the large group of Devil's Psychos turned and walked away, following her brother's order. Only Jason and Nico remained behind with her brother. "Kara." Marcos sighed, running a hand over his head.

"You're an asshole." She spat the words at him once his crew was gone.

Marcos only nodded, all his anger dissipated.

"How long?" she asked. She needed to know.

Marcos shook his head. "Don't do this, Kara."

"How. Long," she snapped, pushing out of Johnny's arms and stepping toward her brother.

"Since I was eighteen," Marcos admitted. "We needed the cash."

Kara froze. Since he was eighteen? She would have been just eight years old then. They'd moved out of Creekton to Mourningside that summer, and Kara had started at the private school that fall.

He had done it for *her*. He had done it all for her.

Marcos watched her warily and sighed again. He stepped toward her and pressed a kiss to her forehead. "I may be a shit brother," he stated softly, "but you will always be important to me." He kissed her cheek before he turned and strode away.

Kara was left speechless, her heart racing and her stomach sinking as she watched her older brother walk away from her without a backward glance.

Chapter Twenty-Four

MARCOS TOSSED AND TURNED all night, thoughts weighing him down: his sister, their relationship, over a decade's worth of lies—all to keep her as far away from this life as possible. All to protect her from the dark dangers of the world. All in vain.

She had fallen into this life anyway and now found herself in the arms of the enemy.

Marcos had no idea how Kara had ended up with Knights Ravagers President Johnny "Mayhem" Taylor as her... boyfriend? Lover? Whatever they were. But he had seen how Kara had leaned back against him, how she'd rested her hands on his. There was no doubt that she trusted him.

Trusted him probably a hell of a lot more than she trusted her own brother at this moment.

He sighed and threw the sheets off. He hadn't slept. Even after he had gotten absolutely shit-faced, landed face-first in bed, and had a club whore suck his cock, he still hadn't slept.

He had ungraciously kicked her out some time around three a.m. only to stare at the ceiling, lost in thought until the sun came up.

He stumbled into the bathroom and took a shower. He zoned out, trying to wake up while the hot water rained down on him. He didn't move until the water turned cold, and only then did he stumble through his hygiene routine.

A half hour later he was on his bike, flying down the road. He needed to clear his head. He needed coffee. He needed to speak to his sister. In that order.

Two hours later, Marcos pulled up to the gates of the Ravager Knights compound. He made sure he had shown up unarmed, pulling over down the road to remove all of his weapons and stashing them in the saddlebags on his Harley.

A quick glance at his watch told him it was just after nine a.m. He hoped like hell his sister was here. He didn't know where she was staying these days. They hadn't talked much since her accident. All he could hope for was that she was at the clubhouse or someone could get ahold of Taylor and let her know he was there.

The men at the gates made him get off his bike at the gate. Marcos watched as one of them parked his girl in the lineup of bikes while two Knights patted him down for weapons. When they didn't find anything, they let him go.

They led him into the clubhouse while one of them called Taylor. "Wait here," the Knight grumbled and pushed Marcos into a chair at the bar.

Marcos didn't have to wait long before Kara and Mayhem came walking out of a back hallway with Devil and Rockstar behind them.

Kara had on a pair of blue jeans and an oversize white T-shirt, probably one of her men's. The front of the shirt was tucked into the waistband of her jeans, the back left loose behind her. Her long blond hair was up in a messy bun and trailed around her face.

As usual, his sister looked beautiful and badass. The tattooed sleeves were a stark contrast against the white shirt. A pair of flip-flops slapped the wood floor as she walked toward him. Her face was guarded, her mask in place.

"Morning, li'l *Manita*," Marcos greeted her. "I brought donuts, but I think the guys on the gate confiscated them."

Kara kept walking toward him, fire in her blue eyes. He didn't even get a chance to block before she swung back her left fist and set it sailing for his face. He heard the crack of bone on bone, felt the hit reverberate through him as his head was forced to the side with the force of her punch before the pain even registered. He never thought he would regret those boxing classes he made her take as a kid.

"Hot damn." One of her Knights laughed.

Marcos groaned as blood filled his mouth. He spat blood on the floor and turned back to his sister as his fingers grazed over his split lip, inspecting the damage. "I deserved that." He nodded at Kara.

His heart broke as he saw the silver lining her eyes. Tears welled there.

"I'm sorry, Kara. I'm sorry I didn't tell you. I wanted you as far from this life as you could get," he said softly. He kept his eyes on his sister, ignoring her three goons behind her.

"W-why are you here?" Her voice cracked as a tear slipped down her cheek.

His heart squeezed in his chest seeing her pain. Knowing he caused it. "There's something you should know... about your father," he started.

She froze, going utterly still. "What about my father?" Her voice turned to stone and she quickly wiped away her tears. He watched her take a deep breath and pull her mask into place, shelving any emotions she might have shown.

Her men moved in closer, ready for anything. To protect her, he realized, even from her own brother. Marcos sighed. "I didn't realize who he was at first. You know I've never met your father after all these years?"

Kara watched him warily and nodded slowly.

"He's been coming around the Psychos' clubhouse for years. He's friends with Buckley. They've been meeting recently to discuss whatever deal they've got going on. I overheard them talking one day," he said, turning to meet Taylor's gaze.

Taylor moved forward, his steel-blue eyes boring into Marcos's. "What the fuck are you talking about?"

"I overheard them talking a couple weeks ago. They didn't know I was there. They were talking about how Vince was framing King to get him locked up. They're trying to make a deal with Las Serpientes to kill Mac Taylor in prison."

Kara gasped and shot a look at Taylor.

Taylor clenched his jaw, his eyes narrowed on Marcos. "How do I know you're speaking the truth. How do I know this isn't another stunt between our clubs to get another hit on us?"

"I haven't had anything to do with that. Buckley's been moving behind my back. The club's fracturing. The guy he sent to spy here? Buckley did that without a vote. The incident in Alabama? Another of Buckley's rogue moves. He's been losing his mind lately."

Taylor stared him down hard.

"Were you involved in Derrick's shooting?" Kara's voice cut through the tense quiet.

Marcos met his sister's eyes and shook his head. "That was Buckley himself. He and his little group of loyalists. He's purposely been keeping me in the dark about his dealings. Me and anyone loyal to me."

"I've got to make a call," Taylor ground out. "Candela, I'll be in touch." He walked toward the office.

Kara looked over her shoulder at him, watching as Rockstar and Devil turned to follow but paused, waiting for her. She waved them on, waiting for them to go. When they closed the door to what appeared to be their church, Kara turned back to Marcos. She frowned and moved closer.

"You're not going to hit me again are you?" Marcos smirked.

She rolled her eyes. "You'd deserve it if I did," she answered, crossing her arms over her chest.

He nodded slowly. "I would, and more." He sighed, rubbing his jaw.

She shook her head. "I know you were trying to protect me, brother." She sighed. "I know you think you were some white knight in my childhood, sending me to private school and paying for everything... and you were. You were my hero when I was a kid, Marcos. I just wish you felt you could have trusted me with the truth."

Marcos let out a long breath. "We could go back and forth a million different times, and over the years, I've questioned myself about telling you. It would have made things a hell of a lot simpler for me when you were older, when there were certain clubs or bars you couldn't go to." He paused and ran his hands over his buzzed head, gathering his thoughts. "At the end of the day, li'l *Manita*,

I would do it all over again. In a heartbeat. You're my baby sister, and I would do anything to protect you."

Kara gave him a watery smile before she wrapped her arms around him and rested her head against his chest. "I love you, big brother."

"I love you too, li'l sister."

Chapter Twenty-Five

JOHNNY CALLED CHURCH THE second Marcos told him that his father was in danger. Las Serpientes were no joke and were not to be messed with. They were a gang of mercenaries and the lowest of scum. They dealt in heroin and human trafficking. Murder for hire was just another day for them.

The Ravager Knights had already gotten Mac Taylor protection inside Mourningside County Correctional when King had first been picked up—Johnny had reached out to the Bratva for protection and reinforced their trade dealings.

Johnny called the Bratva's Pakhan Tarazov before church had started and gave him the heads-up on the potential hit. Tarazov had advised him they would continue to do all they could, but with Las Serpientes, it was not always enough. The Serpents had ways of slipping through the cracks that not even the Bratva could manage.

It hadn't been what Johnny wanted to hear, but he trusted Tarazov enough to see his own hands were tied as well.

During church, Johnny, Derrick, and Kevin brought the club up to speed on what had transpired with Marcos and the division within the Devil's Psychos. They talked about meeting with Marcos and those loyal to him about maybe working with the Psychos to take down Buckley and the rogue crew members.

Buckley's working with Vince Carmichael to frame Mac Taylor was unacceptable. He would need to be dealt with. Now that he was actively attacking the Ravager Knights, he would have to be eliminated. They couldn't allow that level of disrespect to stand.

In the end, they decided to wait. They needed more info, and they needed to see if Marcos and those loyal to him would be willing to help the Knights take out their president.

The next day, Kara was boxing everything up in the dining room at Johnny's house. The case was officially built, and they had what they needed to hand over to the district attorney. Danvers would bring everything to the DA's office in the morning.

They had agreed that, for all intents and purposes, Kara shouldn't go with him to city hall to hand over the case. Kara would need to take over Carmichael and Associates again once her father was arrested. It would be simpler if she aided the case from afar.

District Attorney Lacey Winters wasn't exactly a friend but an acquaintance that Kara respected—trusted to do her job fully. She was smart and damn good at her job. The county was lucky to have her.

There had been several times over the years that Kara had offered her a job in the private sector, offered to pay her well. But each time Winters had turned her down. She had integrity and a strength that Kara admired. Kara trusted she would take the case they were about to hand her and not fumble it. Vince Carmichael would be behind bars by the end of the week.

The last file on the table was the one Danvers had found regarding Marcos's true father. She had given Danvers the original but kept a copy for herself and ones for Marcos and Johnny as well. She was out of time. She needed to present her findings to both men.

She would have to start with Johnny. It was his father. All of this revolved around Mac Taylor.

As if he had read her mind, the back door opened, and she heard three sets of keys hit the counter in the laundry room. Three sets of boots slapped the tile floor before they were slowly pulled off.

She had just finished stacking the last of the boxes when her men came into the great room, Johnny leading them. "Hey, how was your day?" she asked as they came over and greeted her with kisses.

"Long." Johnny sighed, falling heavily into his recliner.

Once Derrick and Kevin had also kissed her, they sat on either end of the long couch. Kara grabbed the manila file folder off the dining room table and headed into the living room area. "Well, I'm only going to make your day even longer." She sighed, stopping in front of Johnny.

He looked up at her grave face and froze. "What happened?" he asked, reaching for the file folder.

She held onto it as she said, "Danvers and I found this when we were digging through everything. There's something I haven't told you about your father from when I visited him in county," she admitted.

Johnny leaned forward and rested his elbows on his powerful thighs. He grabbed the file folder out of her hands but didn't open it. He looked up at her with a narrowed gaze. "What do you mean?"

"I mean lawyer-client privilege. Your father told me something that happened forty years ago that he might not have told you because he didn't know the truth," she hedged, wanting him to understand where she was coming from. The last thing she wanted was for him to be pissed off at her for revealing the truth after all this time.

"Babe, just spit it out. You're killing me here." Johnny groaned, opening the file folder.

Kara saw the words *Paternity Test* and started talking while Johnny read them himself. "Mac and my father told me conflicting stories along similar lines. They were each dating a woman they were in love with, and each might have been engaged to her. Turns out they were dating the same woman and didn't know it. She was cheating on both of them and got pregnant."

"Who was the woman?" Johnny demanded, looking up at her.

"Carlita Candela. My mother," she answered. She didn't look away from Johnny as she heard Kevin gasp. Kevin knew all the details because they had spelled it out together with Jack's help. Kevin didn't know about the pregnancy though.

"What are you saying?" Johnny said, looking back down at the papers in front of him, trying to make sense of it.

"My mother had a son with Mac Taylor. We found the paternity test results in the boxes. You have a brother," she told Johnny.

Johnny tossed the papers on the coffee table and stood up. Kara backed up a step and watched him start to pace the living room. "What the fuck?" He breathed.

"Dude, that's fucked up." Derrick sighed.

Kara met Kevin's gaze. His eyes were wide. He mouthed *Marcos* and she nodded solemnly.

"Who? Your mother? That would mean..." Johnny trailed off and looked at her from across the room.

"Marcos is your half brother," Kara stated, spelling it out for him.

"What the fuck!" Johnny growled and continued his stalking of the living room. "Does he know? Does Candela know?"

Kara sighed. "As far as I know? No, my brother doesn't know. Growing up, he always said we had different dads, but he didn't know *who* his father was."

"Are you sure about that?" Johnny shot back, angry.

She shook her head. "No. I didn't even know my brother was in a motorcycle club until Saturday," she admitted, feeling foolish. How was she supposed to reassure her man that they could trust Marcos when she hadn't even known such a fundamental aspect of who he was as a person until two days ago?

She took a seat on the coffee table so she could watch Johnny stalk the room. She wished she could help him, ease his pain in some way.

"Do we know for sure though? Those documents are forty years old, and you said she lied. Could they be forged?" Johnny asked, grasping at straws.

She smiled sadly. "I don't think those are forged. Those look to be the legit documents from the clinic." She sighed. "We could always have them rerun. Test your DNA against Marcos's."

"Marcos fucking Candela." Johnny growled and shook his head. "Fine." He nodded. "Set up a meeting. We'll discuss it and talk to him about going after Buckley."

"Alright." Kara nodded slowly. "I'll call my brother."

The next day Kara was sitting in the almost empty clubhouse with Johnny. Kevin and Derrick were upstairs in the dorms, giving them privacy. Marcos had agreed to meet in the afternoon, and everyone was on edge because of it.

Too many factors were at play here, too many things were riding on this meeting. Everyone was anxious, Kara included. How the fuck was her hotheaded brother going to take the news that the president of his rival MC was his *father*?

Probably about as well at Johnny had taken the news that he might have a half brother that was the VP of the rival MC that had been shooting at his club. "How are you doing?" Kara asked Johnny.

He was pacing again. A caged lion, ready to fight. He hadn't slept the night before, not really. Even after she went down on him a second time in the middle of the night, he still hadn't slept more than an hour or two.

"I don't know," he admitted, coming to a stop before her.

Kara stood up slowly and went to him, running her hands up his muscular chest. His hands slowly came around her waist and pulled her against him.

"I know we're not related," he hedged, looking down at her. "But does it seem like we are? Is it weird to you? Shit, I should have thought about that last night before I shoved my cock down your throat."

Kara laughed and Johnny finally smiled, relaxing slightly. "It is weird," she admitted, "but not in an incestuous way, more in an 'I can't believe it' way, and don't worry, lover boy. We aren't related, regardless of the fact that we might share a brother."

Johnny grumbled a laugh and kissed her soundly. They were so lost in each other that they didn't hear anyone else come in the barroom until they heard a throat clearing. They stopped kissing and turned their heads to see who was there but otherwise didn't pull apart.

"Sister," Marcos greeted, nodding at Johnny.

"Candela, thanks for coming," Johnny said, holding on to Kara a little tighter.

"Kara said she wanted to talk. That you wanted to talk." Marcos nodded.

Kara smiled at her brother. "I did. We do." She nodded at Johnny, rubbing her hand against Johnny's chest before she slowly pulled away from him. She knew he was anxious, was trying to mask that, and having her near helped calm him, but her brother would not appreciate having a conversation with her if her boyfriend was all over her. "Let's take a seat." She motioned toward one of the many tables in the barroom.

Kara had made up a plate of cheeses and meats, a charcuterie board in a sense, not that she'd ever call it that in front of those big tough bikers. They were too *tough* for something as froufrou as charcuterie. She placed a bottle of Macallan in the center of the table with three glasses and called it good. They weren't picky, and fucking Marcos was lucky she was even feeding him.

Marcos took one look at her little setup and shot her a tentative smile. He could see the olive branch for what it was. She was still pissed at him, still didn't know what to think of his hiding the truth from her her whole life, but she could understand the reasoning.

And she was about to turn his whole world upside down.

So why not a little whisky with his meat and cheese?

"What's going on, li'l *Manita*?" Marcos grumbled, his voice thickly accented.

"As you know, I've been dating Johnny." She started slowly, glancing away. Unable to meet her brother's gaze, she looked down at her hands. She picked up a piece of salami from the platter and twisted it in her fingers. "Along with Kevin and Derrick," she added, needing to get it all out on the table.

Marcos grunted, shifting in his chair. She saw his legs shift under the table but didn't look up at him to see his thoughts.

"They came to me shortly after Mac was arrested and asked for my help," Kara said, finally looking up from the mangled salami slice. "Mac was arrested on charges of racketeering, embezzlement, money laundering, and fraud, accused of using Case Holdings to do it."

"Shit." Marcos groaned and shot a look at Johnny.

Johnny just nodded once, his face stony.

"Long story short," Kara sighed, knowing her brother wouldn't care much about all the other bullshit that was related to her firm, "I've been investigating Case Holdings for the last eight months or so because the name kept coming up in billing reports at the firm. After hiring a forensic accountant and seeing a tech guy and digging through years' worth of case files from forty years ago, we know that Case Holdings was founded by Mac Taylor and my father together. We know that they were best friends and in love with the same woman, probably both engaged to her. We know she cheated on them and lied to them and that she was pregnant." Kara paused and stared at her brother.

Marcos shifted again, eyes narrowing. "What are you saying?"

"I'm saying that Mom was involved with both Vince and Mac forty years ago. I'm saying that she cheated on them with the other and got pregnant. She told Mac it wasn't his child and told Vince it was his. But she got a paternity test done that showed the opposite. When I was digging in the files from back then I found the paternity test." Kara spoke slowly, unable to physically say the words she knew she needed to speak.

How the fuck was she going to tell her brother that his father was Mac Taylor? She tossed the mangled salami onto the table and grabbed a napkin. She twisted the napkin around her greasy fingers, trying to clean them and distract herself.

"Kara." Marcos snapped, glaring at her. He was tired of her pussyfooting around. She needed to spit it out already.

She grabbed the bottle of Macallan and quickly poured out two fingers into each of the three glasses. She looked up at Johnny, who had been watching her warily. He seemed relieved for the whisky though.

Kara looked at Marcos as she slid him the third glass. "Mac Taylor is your father," Kara said evenly, without preamble. But then, the whole fucking conversation had been preamble, hadn't it? She took a long pull from her glass and met her brother's gaze.

Marcos froze, his hand clutching the whisky glass. The muscles in his jaw worked as he ground his molars, his eyes flashing with rage. "Say that again?" He growled.

Tears welled in Kara's eyes. She knew any talk of his father was a sore subject for him. Growing up, he'd always acted so tough, but she knew how it bothered him. Knew he would disappear for hours anytime she brought it up.

"It's true." Johnny grunted, running a hand over his buzzed hair. "I saw the paternity papers myself." He reached behind him to the table where Kara had set the file folder with the test results. Johnny handed them to Marcos.

"Jesus Christ!" Marcos swore and stood up. One look at the papers, with their mother's name next to Mac Taylor's, had him stalking away from the table.

The tears fell down Kara's face as she watched her brother's world crumble. She knew he had the same fantasy she'd had growing up, that deep-down fantasy that a father would appear, would come and save you and give you a better life. Marcos may be forty years old and not a believer in fairy tales anymore, but his world was still shattered.

His father was the president of the rival club that his own club was starting a war with. His father was in jail after being framed by the president of his MC.

Johnny watched Marcos stalk the room with narrowed eyes. He was assessing the man. Assessing a threat or an ally, Kara didn't know. She did know they were short on time. Johnny spoke up before Kara could. "There's more," Johnny stated.

Marcos shot him a look. "More than us sharing the same damn father?" he snapped out.

Johnny shrugged. "We don't have the luxury of hugging it out and doing the brother shit right now. In case you don't remember, your club and president have been attacking me and mine. I already lost one brother recently; I don't plan to lose more."

Marcos glared at Johnny from across the room, a big, bad biker with a menacing dark-as-night glare.

"Marquitos, please," Kara said softly.

His gaze snapped to hers at the mention of the nickname. His eyes softened, seeing the tears on her face. "*Chaparrita.*" He sighed, ran a hand over his dark hair, and swore before he walked slowly back to the table and sat down. "Now what?" he asked.

Johnny leaned forward and rested his forearms on the table. "Now we plan how to take down your president and kill two birds with one stone."

Marcos grinned wickedly. "I'm listening."

Chapter Twenty-Six

K ARA WOULD NEVER FORGET where she was and what she was doing the day everything crashed down around her. She would never forget the last time her world felt normal and things were simple. The one pivotal moment when time and space had no meaning. When she could breathe easy, knowing everyone she loved was safe.

It was that half-assed biker version of a charcuterie board with whisky instead of wine.

It was a forty-year-old paternity test that spelled out the truth.

It was two men she loved more than anything in the world meeting as equals for the first time.

It was a black unmarked police car pulling up in front of the clubhouse.

It was a black-suited corrections officer and Freddy fucking Danvers, walking in side by side.

Kara didn't need to hear what happened. One look at Danvers' grim face told her everything she needed to know.

She had failed.

One look at the tall, gray-haired corrections officer told her her whole world was about to be flipped upside down.

Everyone she loved and cherished was about to be in danger.

Time had no meaning in the moments before all hell broke loose. It neither stood still nor sped up, but her whole world crashed down upon her just the same.

Marcos, Johnny, and Kara stood up to greet Danvers and the suit. Blood rushed in Kara's ears. Her heart pounded. Someone grabbed her hand. Johnny. He squeezed it tightly. "What the fuck is this, Danvers?" Johnny growled.

Kara snapped out of it, took a deep breath, and prepared for crisis.

"The DA filed charges against Vince Carmichael this morning. A warrant was issued for his arrest. Police went to his residence to find he has skipped town. He was tipped off," Danvers said, resigned.

Kara's heart sank. "How?" She gasped, knowing damn well it was anybody's guess.

Danvers shrugged and shook his head. "We don't know. Winters has every cop in the county combing the streets for him... but chances are he's out of the country by now." He sighed.

Johnny growled and turned on the suit. "Who the fuck are you?"

The older man didn't flinch or even look alarmed by Johnny's outburst. He gave a grave nod and held up a file folder with the Mourningside County Correctional seal on the front. "My name is Jim Valen," he introduced himself. "I'm a correctional officer down at Mourningside County Correctional. Are you Johnathan Taylor?"

Johnny could only nod.

Kara squeezed Johnny's hand tightly. She heard movement behind her and glanced over her shoulder to see Kevin and Derrick walking in, clearly having heard the commotion and come to check it out.

Kara turned back to the suit just in time for him to say, "I'm afraid I'm here with bad news. I'm sorry to have to tell you this, but Mac Taylor was killed this morning during a fight in the yard."

Kara's whole world slowed to a stop. Her heart sank to the floor as Johnny let out an animalistic roar. She was pushed aside as he launched himself at the corrections officer. Kevin and Derrick and Marcos tried in vain to hold him back.

Danvers pulled Kara out of the cross fire.

Tears poured down her face as a choking sob shook her body.

She had failed. She had failed. She had failed.

It was her fault. She hadn't found the pieces in time. She didn't build the case fast enough. Her father had gotten away, and Johnny's father was... Oh God. She couldn't breathe.

Johnny was still lunging for the corrections officer. Danvers now tried to help restrain him with the others. The commotion only caused the rest of the Ravager Knights to storm into the barroom of the clubhouse, patched members rushing in to aid their vice president.

Kara could do nothing but watch in despair as her family fell apart.

To be continued...

Did you miss out on Courting the Consequences?
Check it out here!

Choices have consequences, and some consequences cannot be undone.

Fighting to survive is all Kara Carmichael knows. Whether it was surviving the streets as a poor kid on the southside of Mourningside, Illinois or fighting the legal injustices in the court room, Kara prides herself on her ability to fight and win.

She also knows that every choice you make, has an outcome or consequence.

As the managing partner of the most prestigious law firm in the city, Kara had fought her way into a good life. She had made all the right choices.

Or so she thought.

When the Ravager Knights MC rolls into her law firm and kicks up trouble, Kara has a choice to make.

Fight the soul burning attraction of three rough and tumble bikers? Or fight for the prestigious job and gilded lifestyle she worked her entire life building?

Acknowledgements

To my loving husband... your support has been constant and the foundation that allowed me to follow my dreams. From every meal you cooked, to every bedtime with the kids you handled on your own while I met with a writing group, or met a deadline, you have handled without complaint—mostly —and with support. You are my rock and home, always. I love you.

To my best friend, Rachel. Thank you for ALWAYS being my best friend and sister. Your constant support and guidance have been a life-saver over the many years of our friendship. You're always willing to listen to me bather on about writing or life in general. While I've ranted and raved, or whined and cried, you've always supported me without judgment—or with some much needed—and loved me unconditionally. I love you girl.

To my author friend Jessica Baker, thank you for the countless hours of support, brain storm sessions, and encouragement. Thank you for every single piece of wisdom, advice and guidance you've offered me throughout not only the publishing process, but in life in general. Your knowledge and friendship have been an absolute blessing. I will cherish our friendship always.

To my ARC readers! Cici, Shreya, and Laura! Thank you SO so much, from the bottom of my heart! I really appreciate your thoughts and feedback.

M.E. Thornwood is a contemporary romance author, who enjoys writing about dark themes, thrilling suspense, and hot hot spice. She loves her alpha males and the women who don't put up with them. Writing has been her passion since she was a little girl.

She lives in the Midwest with her husband and two children. When she's not writing, she's enjoying camping and hiking with family and friends, crafting with her kids, and reading books with her loveable fat cat Midnight.

www.ingramcontent.com/pod-product-compliance
Lightning Source LLC
Chambersburg PA
CBHW022110310726
48972CB00007B/1977